Jesus and the Art of Scuba Diving

INDIGORIVER
PUBLISHING

Jesus *and* *the* Art *of* Scuba Diving

A NOVEL

JAMIE ROBBINS

Jesus and the Art of Scuba Diving

This is a work of fiction. Unless otherwise indicated, all the names, characters, businesses, places, events, and incidents in this book are either the product of the author's imagination or used in a fictitious manner. Any resemblance to actual persons, living or dead, or actual events is purely coincidental.

Editors: Charlotte Chipperfield, Stephanie Thompson
Cover and Interior Design: Emma Elzinga

Indigo River Publishing
3 West Garden Street, Ste. 718
Pensacola, FL 32502
www.indigoriverpublishing.com

Ordering Information:

Quantity Sales: Special discounts are available on quantity purchases by corporations, associations, and others. For details, contact the publisher at the address above.

Orders by US trade bookstores and wholesalers: Please contact the publisher at the address above.

Printed in the United States of America

Library of Congress Control Number: 2025911849
ISBN: 978-1-964686-65-3 (paperback) 978-1-964686-66-0 (ebook)

First Edition

As a scuba instructor I have the opportunity to see fear changed to courage, faintheartedness converted into accomplishment, timidity transformed into confidence, and anticipation turned into a passion. As a scuba instructor I can open hearts and minds to the hidden beauty of nature's creation and our obligation to protect it, foster self-esteem in another person, teach the value of character and integrity, and transform another human being and change a life for the better and forever.

— Professional Association of Diving Instructor's (PADI) creed

FOREWORD

When Jamie honored me with an invitation to write this foreword, I thought it was because I'm passionate about Jesus and because I'm passionate about diving, with a career in the latter. Having had a chance to read early drafts of *Jesus and the Art of Scuba Diving*, that made sense.

Both diving and Christianity transform you in positive but different ways. In the broad view, they are disconnected. True, some people and groups dive together because they also worship together, but obviously, diving doesn't require faith in Christ. Diving is not tied to any religion. The Professional Association of Diving Instructors—PADI, the world's dominant diver training organization, where I have worked for almost forty years—is silent and neutral regarding faith. This is appropriate considering that annually, PADI certifies hundreds of thousands of divers from virtually every belief, culture, and country.

So, like everything I do, my walk with Christ influences my diving. But I never saw it the other way around, with diving significantly shaping my life as a Christian.

Until I read *Jesus and the Art of Scuba Diving*.

What hits hard in this novel is the transformation one experiences as *both* a follower of Christ *and* a diver. It has its own kind of transformation. The story exemplifies that Jesus amazingly transforms us into something greater than the sum of the parts we give him to work with—if we let him.

This story is not an easy read. Don't get me wrong, it's interesting and reads quickly, but much of it is based on unimaginably difficult events in Jamie's real life. His characters ask frank, uncomfortable faith-related questions. They dialog in ways that make us squirm; if we're honest, they demand answers. You likely won't agree with all the characters' statements and conclusions, but don't worry. You're not supposed to. Real truth stands up to questioning, and you'll come away with more to pray about, more insight into yourself and Jesus, and more strength in your faith. So that means this story is transformative for readers too.

So, while I'm passionate about Jesus and diving, maybe that's not what Jamie was thinking about when he asked me write this foreword. Perhaps what Jamie saw, and what I'd been almost blind to until I read his book, was a single ongoing transformation that transcends these passions. And perhaps that's something you will discover too.

Karl Shreeves
PADI Education and Content Development Executive

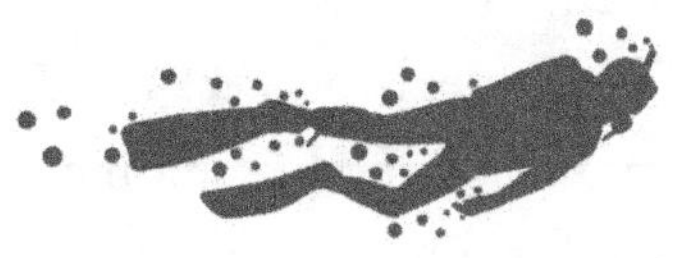

1

Panic underwater always starts in the eyes—wide open, pupils dilated, flicking from side to side, scanning the environment but seeing nothing. Mark, my student, is still learning to dive, and he is beginning to panic. I grab his arm and pull him close, face-to-face. He seems to be staring at me, but somehow, he's gazing right through me. I know from a handful of other experiences that Mark sees nothing.

Dammit, I'm thinking to myself, *Here we go again*. In my twenty-five years of teaching scuba diving to hundreds of students, I'd seen it all before. And still, I'm not sure why my first thought is anger.

I search his face for clues as to what will happen next as he spits the breathing regulator from his mouth like rotten fruit and rips the mask off his face. He's screaming into the water as he begins to surface. The screaming, oddly, is a welcome sign to me that he's not holding his breath, which could permanently damage his lungs as trapped air expands on his ascent. Contrary to popular belief, sound travels well underwater, and he is roaring.

He rips his arm from my hand. I grab at anything I can reach on his equipment and pull him close to my body. I wrap my legs around his to keep him from kicking and ascending too quickly. I glance down at my two other students waiting on the sandy bottom of these clear, warm Hawaiian waters. They squint into their masks to get a better look at their father, who is ending yet another dive in panic. I look back at Mark. The muscles in his neck flex. He was probably an athlete in his day. He is strong, and he's putting up a good fight. He would be fighting me off in a more coordinated manner if he were in his right mind, but his reasoning brain has shut down, as it does for everyone in fight or flight mode. His mask falls between us, and I manage to catch it in my left hand...more luck than skill. When students fully panic, which is not often, their instinct is to get their head above water as fast as they can.

I wrap my legs even more tightly around his. He's clawing at the water like a trapped animal trying to scratch its way to the surface. One of his outstretched talons catches the edge of my mask and rips it from my face. We are both in a haze of bubbles. I can feel my mask settle under my chin, the strap stretched around my neck. I dismiss the instinct of self-preservation to let go of Mark and place the mask back on my face. The water around us is clouded, and panic begins to gnaw at the edges of my brain. We could easily lose sight of the surface. I know that if I can gain control of the situation, both of us will be okay. I can no longer see, but I can feel we're moving toward the surface because the pressure in my ears is ebbing. I refocus my brain on the situation, and an odd, peaceful feeling washes over me. Time slows to a crawl. My brain, like Mark's, has entered an altered state. Panic has dulled his vision, but I gain a keen sense of our surroundings. Based on his actions, Mark has lost his mind. I've somehow found mine.

I hear my son crying out from the depths to save Mark. It shakes me. It's never happened before, and I don't have time to sort this out in my mind. I want to stop and listen to the voice of my dear, long-lost son, but I must focus on the more pressing goal here: Get us both safely out of this nightmare. Losing my son has stalled my life in a way and crushed my desire to create new adventures. At the same time,

I've also become a man who now finds his only peace in the midst of chaos that drowns out my pain. And that is where I am with Mark... in the depths of chaos.

He breaks through the surface, dragging me with him. Moments later, bobbing on the water, he has no recollection of how he got there. He doesn't say anything at first. He just stares to the east.

I glance off into the direction he's staring and see our dive boat, the *Hihi'o* (hee-hee-oh), waiting patiently about a hundred yards away in the sparkling clear water off Hawaii's Big Island. The one-hundred-and-ten-foot boat is anchored near a spot called Turtle Pinnacle, considered by most to be an easy dive. Aqua water laps gently against the sides of the boat as a half dozen divers from another group make their way up twin aluminum ladders hanging off the stern. Today is our first day aboard the *Hihi'o*, and it will be home for a week, off the Kona coast, for me, my three students, and twenty-eight other divers.

The serenity of the clear, blue Hawaiian water contrasts sharply to my experience with Mark. Mark's adult son and daughter slowly surface near us and inflate their buoyancy compensators, also known as BCs, as I taught them earlier. In addition to providing buoyancy, their BCs fit around them as a vest that holds their scuba tanks in place on their backs and lead weights in pouches under their arms. His daughter Olivia looks our way. Her mouth begins to move, but no words come out. I attempt to return her gaze, but she is not looking at me. I've been working with the three of them for about a week, and this is the first time I've seen her without a smile on her face. Her brow furrows as she continues to stare at her father Mark. Her brother, Jason, is looking at me expectantly, awaiting my next instruction.

"Let's head back to the boat," I finally say. "You can swim on your backs or snorkel in...whatever you prefer."

Silently, we all lay back and kick our fins to slowly push us back toward the boat. I had been in a pool for two days with this family, starting about a week ago, then shore diving for two more days prior to our boat trip. Jason and Olivia had easily mastered their skills to earn their Open Water Diver certification, but Mark was still struggling. The three had elected to continue their dive training journey by joining me on a live-aboard dive boat complete with sleeping accommodations and a dining room, also called a salon. My hope was to finish Mark's certification at the beginning of our boat trip then move on to the Advanced Open Water Diver course with the three of them throughout the week. I continue to check on Mark as we swim. Jason and Olivia reach the ladders while Mark and I are still fifty feet away. Mark looks over to me and we lock eyes. His pupils constrict as he searches my face.

"Hey, Morgan...what just happened?" he says, calling me by my last name.

"How are you feeling?" I ask.

"Man, I just couldn't get my bearings."

"You panicked and bolted for the surface," I say, answering his first question.

His grimace tells me he's either in pain or confused, maybe both. He tilts his head to the right and shakes some water from his ear.

"Those dramatic pressure changes from fast ascents can do a number on your ears," I say.

He tilts his head back up straight and gently shakes it as if trying to comprehend what I'm saying.

"Wow, I have no idea what just happened," he says. "How deep were we?"

"Only about twenty feet. That's why we do our skills in relatively shallow water. Just in case." I hand him back his mask that I happened to snag on our way to the surface. He says nothing as the dazed look in his eyes begins to fade and he no longer appears to be looking through me.

"Well, Mark, it's not uncommon for people to become disoriented underwater and then panic."

Mark blinks again. His gaze shoots over my shoulder toward the *Hibi'o*. "Yeah," is all he says.

"They spit their regulators out, pull their masks off, and swim to get to the—"

"Is it lunchtime yet?" Mark interrupts, returning his gaze to me.

"Probably." I smile, trying to squelch my frustration. "Let's get back to the boat."

"Stop thinking about that," he says as we near the boat.

"What did you say?" I ask.

"Nothing...just talking to myself," he replies.

I can guess what is running through his mind. He is trying to understand fear and panic. I've seen this before over the years. I have taught many students how fear can never really be eliminated. It can be mastered and even used to your advantage. But when fear, often manifesting as panic, is allowed to take control of the decision-making process, bad things happen.

The combination of the physicality, the emotional discipline, and the technical thought process of diving is what has always made it much more than just a recreational activity to me. Since I was fifteen years old, diving has been a way to interpret the world around me. Diving was a way of placing myself outside of normal human activity and continually pushing myself away from comfort toward a truer perspective of my life. Even after all these years under the water, moments still arise when I feel panic and fear creeping into my consciousness. I have learned to control those feelings, but they never completely go away. Having that mind control also protects me from darker thoughts since tragedy entered my life.

I know what drives me to continue learning and teaching. I understand fear and panic and how they can be mastered, and I enjoy teaching that to others. But, at the same time, I am frustrated by the process. I don't really understand the conflicted feelings I experience. Would this student, Mark, complete the last skill necessary for his diving certification? I always remain hopeful, but I know some will never complete the steps to learn diving. I have the same feeling about my life. Would I finally embrace the lessons to carry on with my journey or remain stuck in grief, hoping my life could somehow be shortened?

There are so many steps to getting a dive certification. My hope is to help Mark complete the one skill he had left to master: removing, replacing, and clearing the water from his mask. We are nearing the boat, and I remember a conversation I had with him during his pool training a week ago...

"My girlfriend told me about the dangers of diving," Mark said as we toweled off after his last pool session in the prior week. "My sister said the same thing."

"Did they have a bad experience diving?" I asked as I dried my face.

"My brother-in-law did," Mark said. "He never really told me what it was, but he was all over the place mentally anyway. He's been in addiction recovery programs, churches, cults, self-help seminars, Eastern religions...you name it, he's tried it."

His description of his brother-in-law made me wonder if Mark was also talking about himself. He told me his brother-in-law's inability to overcome whatever it was that had a hold of him had him constantly seeking a solution or a means to fix what he might have been going through. Mark has hinted to me that he too is going through something. I'm trying to figure it out because this fear seems to have taken over and almost seriously injured him or even cost him his life today. My head is reeling as we continue to swim to the boat.

"Hey, Morgan," Mark snaps at me. "The boat's this way." He jabs his thumb over his shoulder to indicate I was swimming a bit off course. I'm not sure why he chose early on to call me by my last name instead of my given name John, but it somehow feels appropriate. I hear him and change course, but my mind continues to drift a bit as I think about Mark, his brother-in-law, and many other diving students. The pattern of fear leading to panic leading to bad decisions just continues over and over for some. All of the inner demons come out underwater, where rational thought can be drowned. But rational thought has to be preserved if this student is to survive and master his fear.

Upon arriving at the boat, Mark grabs ahold of the ladder and fumbles with a gloved hand to remove one of the straps on his fins. I steady him from behind as he begins to teeter on the ladder in the wake of a passing boat.

"Slow down," I offer. "Just take your time. There's no rush."

"I can never get these dammed things off my feet," he says, ignoring my comment and pulling harder to remove his fin.

I had advised him in the dive shop to look at fins with a bungee cord strap that were easy to slip over his heel. He liked the other, less-expensive fins with a snap-clasp, quick-release that works great with bare fingers while standing next to the display counter. Finding the release with gloved hands while hanging from a ladder in a rolling swell is a different story. He breaks free of his first fin and attempts to hand it to a waiting crew member on the swim step. The fin drops out of his hand, hits the swim step on the boat, and bounces off my head and into the water. I grab it and toss it onto the swim step, along with his mask I had already returned to him twice during our swim. I wondered if he was trying to lose his mask on purpose as an excuse to end his dive training.

"Oh, sorry about that, Morgan," he says as he unclips his second fin. He manages to keep a grip on this fin and hands it to the crew member. He places a foot on the ladder and begins to climb, leaning dangerously to one side, his substantial weight seeming to bend the ladder sideways. I am exhausted but grateful everyone in my group is back on the *Hibi'o*. Mark is a bit taller than me—probably around six-two, judging from when I helped him into a wetsuit at the start of our course. He had maintained his rugged good looks over the years with a tanned face, angular chin, penetrating blue eyes, and a dashing smile. On the other hand, he had the body of a former college football player who had stopped playing the sport but kept eating as if he hadn't quit.

"Both feet on the ladder before you climb," I caution from behind. I've told him this several times, but his desire to get out of the water overrides my instructions. He ignores me again and sways back and forth up the ladder. I stay to one side so he at least won't land on me if he slips and falls backward. Once he is on deck, I quickly remove my fins while still in the water, put the straps over my wrists, and begin a weary climb up the ladder as the fifty pounds of gear on my back attempts to pull me off the rungs. I notice Olivia and Jason are already back on deck and out of their gear.

The crew directs us to open seats in front of tank racks in the aft part of the boat. I don't know the official name of that area, but I like to call it the dive deck. We wipe the snot from our faces as we wriggle out of the shoulder straps on our scuba kits and unburden ourselves of the heavy air tanks and lead weights.

"Does that count as dive number four?" Mark asks me as we sit on the benches.

"I'm afraid not," I reply. "A safe ascent is part of the dive."

"I figured," Mark says. "Not sure I'm ever going to finish this course."

"Every natural instinct you have underwater is wrong and can get you in serious trouble if you let it," I say. "Remember? That was one of the very first things I said to you." As the words escape my lips, I can hear a harsh tone in my comment.

"Yeah, I remember," he admits. "It's just hard to remember underwater when the voice in my head is screaming, 'You can't breathe! You can't see! You're going to die if you don't get out of here!'"

I say nothing. My sympathetic side is begging me to somehow console him, but I have observed over the years that students have to first work through failure in their own minds before arriving at the idea of getting back into the water. While their bodies say "no more," their minds can push them forward. I won't offer encouragement until Mark fully absorbs the idea he had failed.

"I'll always encourage you to try again," I say. "And I'll try with you as many times as you want to...but I can't make you *want to* do anything. And you really have to *want to* finish this course."

He stares at me blankly.

"You did great on that dive," his daughter Olivia says as she approaches where we are sitting. She is sincerely trying to be encouraging. Olivia exudes positive energy. She has a towel wrapped around her waist and weaves her dirty blonde hair into a loose braid. She's an eager learner. She and Jason have already completed their mandatory four Open Water dives and associated skills in the past couple of days with seemingly little or no trouble. They both had become certified scuba divers.

"What happened?" Jason asks, stepping from behind his older sister and placing his hand on his father's shoulder while adjusting his board shorts with the other. "Mask stuff?"

"Yeah, mask stuff," Mark replies. "For some reason I can put a little water in my mask or even flood it completely and still keep it together long enough to clear the water back out. But when I take that damned thing completely off my head, I just lose it."

"But you swam underwater in the pool with no mask on like the rest of us and did fine," Olivia says. "I'm sure you can do it."

"Obviously you didn't see the end of the dive then," Mark shoots back.

"It looked like you may have gone up a bit too quickly, but I couldn't see you clearly," she says.

"Well, according to Morgan here," he says, jabbing his thumb in my direction, "we don't get participation awards. We do the skills correctly or we do them over again. Close doesn't cut it. In case you didn't notice, he's not the most sympathetic guy."

"My wife says I was in the wrong line when compassion was handed out," I say in a failed attempt to add some levity. "Probably true, but I know from my years of teaching experience that sympathy will short-circuit the process in this part of his journey."

The tension continues to rise in our little group, and I hear my wife Mary telling me to take it down a notch. She has always been the voice of reason in my life, whether or not I wanted to hear it. She remains my constant companion while contending with her own grief over losing our son years before. Olivia shoots me a quizzical look as if she's trying to get me to say something or maybe just get me to stop saying anything. I'm not great at taking hints, but I begin to infer, as she nods toward Mark, that she's telling me to try her tactic and encourage her dad.

"I'll leave you two to do your post-dive debriefing," she says as she turns and walks away. Jason deftly steps aside for his sister, then silently follows her into the salon, a spacious air-conditioned cabin toward the front of the boat. The indoor space is filled with tables, chairs, banquette seating along the side walls, and a central galley where all of the meals are prepared. Jason never says much and remains a bit of a mystery to me. I watch him walk behind his sister, and I'm envious of his apparent ability to eat everything in sight yet keep his collegiate lacrosse lean and muscular frame. Normally I would debrief the whole group after a dive, but perhaps the fact that Mark and I are left alone as the other divers on the boat begin to meander into the salon is a good thing. I decide to break it down alone with Mark.

I don't say it, but I'm wondering if Mark will get past this mask skill or just give in to the false pretense of "at least I tried." I have taught many to scuba dive, but I know I am really in the business of transformation. From the first breath underwater in a shallow pool to diving sixty feet under the waves just days later is a big change in a very short time. For some it is a subtle change. For others like Mark, who are stuck somewhere in their mind, it will be monumental. I'd seen it many times while peering into the masks of students over the years. I could somehow see the gears turning in their minds as they tried to comprehend this new and very unfamiliar environment. For my students to learn to scuba dive, they first have to learn to overcome their natural responses to danger and perceived danger—logic has to override their instincts. I could teach their minds the logical steps of learning to dive, but they would be required to relay that information to their bodies.

Understanding something intellectually is very different from doing something physically. Their reasoning selves reside in the frontal lobes of their brains, making logical, organized, and thoughtful responses. But their bodies often respond to stressful circumstances from the limbic cortex, the lizard brain, where things like panic, primal fear, and addiction reside. The only way to progress is to simply stop reacting to everything around them and teach their logical brains to override their instincts. I would teach my students to repeat the mantra, "I'm OK. I can breathe. Now, what do I need to do next?"

Mark and I peel off our wetsuits as we sit on the dive deck in the sun. Mark tells me he was thinking about his life as we were swimming back to the boat. He was thinking about how he lived his life much in the same way he dove.

"Fear and panic are normal human responses to many things that happen in life," he says. "Everybody panics once in a while, right?"

"I suppose," I reply while rubbing another layer of sunscreen into my reddening skin. "But panic while diving can get you killed, sometimes quickly, and sometimes slowly."

"What am I even doing out here in the middle of the ocean thinking I can breathe underwater?" Mark mutters. He grabs the sunscreen from me and squirts a dab into his hand.

"I had a student once tell me that diving pushed him to think about how fear kept him from pursuing his dreams and how panic forced him to abandon his fledgling small business and return to the corporate world," I say.

I grab the sunscreen back out of his hand. The SPF 40 gets snatched back and forth between us like some sort of *talking stick* in a communication seminar. But instead of fostering communication, the plastic bottle becomes the talisman of conversational wrestling. This dive debriefing has turned into a philosophical debate.

"He told me he wanted to push himself to learn diving to see if he could master his fear of the ocean and maybe get control of his other fears in life," I continue.

Mark straightens and throws me a sharp glance. I detect rising anger from the look on his face. Then he turns and gazes back out over the ocean. "Maybe that makes sense." He sighs, and his shoulders slump.

"What do you dream of doing?" I ask.

"Wow, nice segue, Morgan. So, you're not talking about some random guy you taught to dive. You're talking about me," he says. "You're not as subtle as you think."

"I'm talking about many people I've taught to dive. You're not much different, but I am trying to ask you a legitimate question here. I don't have a preconceived answer. I don't know you all that well—I'm just asking a question."

He looks me in the eye to see if I am actually interested in his story. "Not much anymore," he finally says.

"Then what did you used to dream?"

Mark tilts his head to the side. "I don't remember exactly, but my life dream certainly wasn't to put in all those hours at the office to fall short of becoming vice president of marketing for a product I don't even care about." He stands abruptly. I look him in the eye, waiting and wondering where he's going with this, but he says nothing. Instead, he turns and walks off toward the showers.

I'm picking up on a theme in our conversations. Based on what he had told me the past week or so, he had not seen many of his dreams through to fruition...would he ever? I often wonder why certain people sign up to learn to dive. They don't seem to enjoy the process much. Some fight through to the end, despite their hesitancy, and others throw in the towel. I don't know if diving was one of Mark's dreams or if he even knows why he signed up for a class.

"He always does this," Olivia says as she approaches me from the salon with a water bottle in hand. She sits down on the bench next to me. "He gets super close to a goal, then something happens. He always falls short of his goals when fate or circumstance seemingly turns against him. He just gives up and moves on to the next challenge. He tried competitive cycling for a while—he was a lot thinner back then—but he had a crash and gave up. He was also actually a pretty competitive golfer for a guy of his age, but he had an argument with his golf pro and quit."

There's something about being out on the ocean, especially in a place where mobile phones don't work, that gets people talking to each other. There are few distractions, other than the diving itself, and a familiarity grows among those on board. There is another layer of familiarity that sometimes grows with my students. They are literally entrusting their lives to me. They must trust that what I am teaching them and where I am taking them won't get them killed. The side effect is a bond that naturally grows between us...a bond typically broken when we return to the dock and I wish them the best with their new diving life.

"I sometimes wonder if that's why our mom left him," Olivia continues.

"Your mom left him?" I ask.

"What's that look on your face, Morgan?" she asks. "You look surprised or something?"

"Nothing. Well, I'm learning you don't hold back much."

She shrugs off my comment. "Yeah, thirty-five years of marriage and he just gives up. I don't know...maybe they both just gave up... depends on who you ask. He also had that girlfriend for a while after that, but he gave up on her too. There always seems to be an element of fear in every corner of his life. He says it's anger, but I think it's fear. I think he's been fearful since his childhood. He had this "thing" happen to him when he was ten, but he won't talk about it. He told me once but swore me to secrecy."

"OK, now I'm really curious."

"Sorry, Morgan. You'll have to drag that one out of him. He'd be pissed to know I even mentioned that something happened to him." She stands, shoots me an engaging smile, and walks forward along the narrow passage on the side of the boat between the railing and the salon. I saw Jason walk that way earlier and surmise she is planning to join her brother on the bow, just forward of the salon. Olivia, unlike her father, stays in fantastic shape. She's not attractive in a glamour magazine sort of way, but she has the fit, muscular body and efficient movements of an athlete. Her wavy, dirty blonde hair is typically pulled loosely back from her constantly smiling face. She has her father's blue eyes and penetrating gaze that can be quite disarming. I've watched as other bikini-clad women on the boat have turned men's heads as they walk by. Olivia doesn't seem to have the same effect, and something tells me she doesn't want to. But when she turns her gaze on me, it's hypnotic—I pay attention. Watching her interact with other divers on the boat, I readily see she has that same effect on others as well.

Mark emerges from the salon and traces Olivia's steps toward the bow. Sitting alone on the dive deck, I ponder how this day is going to end in another defeat for Mark...just one more in a long line of losses. He told me he doesn't want to dive anymore today, but he'll take another shot tomorrow. I'm willing to continue taking the journey with him, but only he can decide how far he wants to go. I watch as Mark walks to the bow and says something to Olivia and Jason before the three of them walk back toward the dive deck and turn to enter the salon. As others make their way in, it dawns on me that lunch is being served. I quickly towel off and slip into shorts, a T-shirt, and flip-flops in the small changing room near the dive deck.

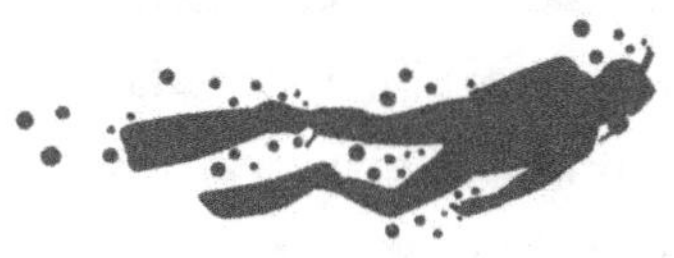

2

I join my little group at their usual table in the salon on the port side across from the galley. We're surrounded by all of the other divers on the boat who are beginning to file through the buffet lunch of various enchiladas, beans, rice, tortilla chips, mango slices, and an impressive array of salsas set out on the galley counter. I sense my group is waiting for the line to taper off a bit before joining the others.

"You looked annoyed or mad or...something when we were swimming back to the boat," Mark says as we stand to get in the buffet line.

"How so?" My jaw clenches.

"When we were swimming back after the dive, you looked mad or something," he repeats. "I don't know, it looked like you were grinding your teeth and talking to yourself. Kinda like you're doing right now. Were you mad at me for panicking?"

I let his question hang in the air without responding. He turns away from me toward the line as it starts to move. We begin to load food onto our plates.

I was angry, and I'm still angry. I don't know why. My first thought when he panicked was a flash of anger. I wasn't mad at him, so what was I mad about? I'd seen people struggle learning to dive before. I can't say anger was my typical response, so why was I mad now? I really wanted Mark to succeed here. I wonder if my anger has more to do with me than him. I, like Mark, felt stuck in my life. Losing my son was confusing in many ways. Things that used to seem important to me—work, money, relationships—now seemed trivial somehow. I had started a few businesses over the years, all of which seemed to be on autopilot these days. Now, the most traumatic event of my life was pushing me into becoming something else...but what?

I tell my students that learning to scuba dive is very unnatural, and a "transformation" of sorts has to happen. Diving is a strange hybrid of natural activity (breathing and swimming), technology (breathing apparatus), and science (decompression theory). They will go from not really believing they can breathe underwater to trusting with their lives that they can. Some make the transition easily. Some never make it. Most struggle somewhere in between. They move from standing upright, held down by gravity, to floating horizontally, held up by buoyancy. They switch from breathing primarily through their noses to breathing through their mouths. They learn to relieve the pressure in their ears caused by the weight of the water pressing in all around them. They shift from walking with pressure on the bottom of their feet to kicking fins with pressure on the tops of their feet. They become very aware of their breathing, and it can no longer just be a reflex activity.

Breathing is really the key to the whole process of becoming a diver. Proper breathing makes buoyancy control easier, squelches panicky feelings by removing carbon dioxide from the body, and feeds the logical brain with fresh oxygen. Breathing begins innately at birth, but learning how to breathe properly underwater is a learned process.

Most people change throughout their lives, but only some are truly transformed. Change is often a choice. Transformation almost never is...at least not after the initial choice. Change is about adapting to life's ups and downs. Transformation is about walking through a process to a destination that is unimaginable.

Mark and I return to our table in the galley area, loaded plates in hand. Olivia and Jason are sitting at the table and are already halfway through their lunches. No one is talking.

"I'm mad about the process of transformation," I finally say in response to Mark's question.

"What the hell does that mean?" he asks, stuffing a large chunk of enchilada into his mouth. Again, I don't answer. He continues to chew as he begins talking to Olivia about potentially taking a nap. I remain silent and can feel tension rising within me. I'm still feeling out of sorts, and I don't know why. Scuba diving, being on boats, teaching this sport to others is where I find peace, not tension.

Olivia looks at me. Her gaze shifts to Mark, and she starts to say something, but no sound escapes her lips.

"A nap sounds good to me," Jason says as he stands. Diving is oddly strenuous, and daytime naps on dive boats are common. He grabs his plate and glass and returns them to the counter. Olivia silently follows her brother, dishes in hand. Mark remains at the table eating his lunch. Jason and Olivia begin to descend the spiral stairway to the bunk room.

How do I explain this to Mark? Transformation is not so much something to be explained as it is something to be experienced. It is typically set into motion by the one being transformed, but it's impossible to maintain control of the process soon after the initial step. Diving can be a catalyst for this process. Change can often be managed—transformation cannot.

I start many of my diving classes by asking students to tell everyone their first name, where they're from, and what they do. I also ask, "Why scuba?" The answers are typically *because my friends, family, or significant other want me to dive with them* or *it's something I've always wanted to try* or *I'm going on a trip to the tropics and want to dive.* No one ever says, "Because I want to see transformation in my life," even though I know that is the real answer. Something in each one of them made them cross the threshold from thinking about diving to signing up for a class…the secret prayer.

The secret prayer is really the desire of the heart. It is a prayer so deeply ingrained in the human psyche that it is not usually recognized as a prayer. This is the prayer of inner longing. It is not saying grace at a Thanksgiving meal. This is a prayer that has nothing to do with religion or church or clergy or any type of learned behavior. This is a prayer that comes up from the darkness of the soul into the light of day.

I've tried to explain it to students in the past, and nobody has ever understood what I meant. Instead, they question what type of lunatic they've selected as their diving instructor.

"I'm not sure I can explain what I mean," I say, slowly spreading mango salsa over what's left of my enchilada.

Mark shrugs and becomes far more interested in his lunch than our conversation. He has no idea what he signed up for with me. I'm betting he thought scuba looked like a fun activity and something to do on vacation with his son and daughter. It may never become a passion for him as it has always been for me. No one seems to know the actual statistics, but many students do not continue to dive after being certified—too expensive, too busy, too cold, too much effort, ear problems, no one to dive with, just not for me, etc.

I suspect that the real reasons many do not continue with diving are the same reasons they don't stay married or committed to friendships or show up for anything consistently—risk, cost, effort, and uncomfortable feelings.

Transformation is a longing in everyone, but few walk it through to the end. It is a painful, difficult, slow process that will always be the most rewarding and least fun part of your life. You can start the process, and you can sometimes stop it, but you cannot alter it. You may want a child someday, but becoming a parent is an unimaginable experience until it happens. You become a different person. For some, it is a natural transition. Others never seem to reach the destination, longing for a past life they can never have again. Some never navigate the many obstacles of a committed relationship to reach the safe harbor of a lifelong partnership. Still others give up amidst the difficulties of becoming a new business owner, right before they may have reached success. Transformation is painful, but there is an unusual beauty and freedom on the other side of it.

"You accidentally said a prayer that started all of this," I say to Mark as he takes a gulp of water. I'm trying to select which one of many thoughts crowding my mind might be most helpful to him.

"I said a prayer?" he responds. "Look, I know you're some kinda religious guy or something, but that's not me. I don't like church, I don't like Christians, and I really don't see the point of any religion other than trying to be a good person."

"That's not what I meant," I say. "I think prayer is a misused word. I don't really think prayer is begging God to do something or get me through a tight spot. I also don't think real prayer is something that can be taught by a church or a religion or learned from your parents. True prayer comes up from within…it's unstoppable. We have certain desires of the heart planted inside of us by—I don't know, I call it God, but you might call it something else."

"You know that's a bunch of bullshit thought up by weak-minded people who can't take responsibility for their lives," he says.

"That's why I don't bring this up anymore. Seems like this conversation never goes anywhere," I say. "Sorry, I know 'prayer' is a loaded word."

Mark stares at me, giving no facial cues as to what he might be thinking. I watch people closely as I teach them to dive. I see the doubt written on the faces of many as they weigh the ramifications of continuing to push themselves versus just calling it quits. I easily see the correlation between overcoming the natural fears of learning to dive and the obstacles of any worthwhile endeavor. I see people getting on and off the ride, but the more I try to explain the connection, the crazier I sound. People write me off as some religious dude or Jesus-freak and don't seem to hear what I'm saying.

"I'm going to the head," Mark announces as he stands, clears his dishes, and slowly walks away to the tiny restroom. He leaves me sitting alone at the table. I sit there wondering why I bring this up. The conversation always ends the same way, with me sitting alone—somewhere between religious folks who write me off as heretical and atheists who dismiss me as delusional. I don't feel sorry for myself. But I do feel frustrated that this process I see is so deeply ingrained in my soul and yet so impossible to explain. I say "frustrated," but it's more like anger. And there we have it—now I know why I got angry when Mark panicked on me. Too bad I won't be able to explain it to him.

I know he said *the prayer* or he wouldn't be here. He would try to convince me otherwise, but I already knew too much about his life. A week before our boat trip, Olivia had one too many beers with our little group in a local bar after one of our swimming pool sessions and began openly questioning her father while I watched.

"Don't you have a desire to see the world or experience all the adventure that traveling can bring?" she asked him that night. "Don't you want to go to Antarctica someday?" Olivia had told me that she and Jason had had much grander experiences than Mark, traveling the world through school and other opportunities.

"Not really," he said. "I have so much adventure in my life right now, I'm not sure I could handle much more." The words felt insincere to me. He had told me his life was exciting in some sense of the word, but certainly not in the way he expected. He always imagined adventure on the high seas as a child, he had told me, but not adventure trying to navigate a marriage, a career, and raising children. Olivia said she "wasn't buying his answer."

Contrary to what he was telling me, Olivia explained, Mark had once considered himself a thoughtful man—a man of deep, inward reflection and even prayer. But since his divorce, he has questioned the idea of what he considered prayer. He had been taught the value of prayer by his grandmother, but in truth, he had never really understood the purpose of prayer in his life. Was he really talking to God or just talking to the wall in his bedroom? Was the voice he heard in response really the Almighty or just a convoluted mass of thoughts collected over a lifetime of overthinking everything said to him and everything that had happened to him?

Olivia had also told me, during a lunch break during one of our pool sessions, her dad and mother divorced while she was away at college. It would have struck me as odd that she was sharing so many details of their family, but it had happened to me many times before while teaching scuba as part of the bond that seems to form quickly between instructor and student. I also tend to ask people a lot of questions—a hold-over from the decade I had spent as a newspaper reporter before joining a startup company in Silicon Valley and eventually starting my own businesses in the tech sector. As Olivia had relayed to me, they married young, had kids, and used to go to church together as a family. But that all ended with the divorce. Her mom married another man who neither Jason nor Olivia liked very much, and God, church, and religion all drowned in the wake of the divorce. Mark hung on to his job and the house but seemed to be adrift at the same time.

Mark returns from the head and clasps the back of his chair as if he's about to sit down. His eyes flick to me, and he lets go of the chair. "I think I need some fresh air," he says.

He heads toward the dive deck at the stern of the boat. It's a beautiful afternoon in the tropics. He fiddles with his gear then climbs the ladder to the sun deck, where about half of the divers on the boat seem to spend most of their afternoons.

Olivia emerges from the stairway she had descended only minutes earlier. I watch as she walks through the salon on her way to the dive deck. She stops in her tracks and turns to look at me. Her brow furrows as a thought crosses her mind. Staring at me, she walks toward my table and plops down in the chair next to me.

"What happened to the nap?" I ask.

"Since the day we met, I keep getting the feeling that I know you from somewhere before," she says with a smile, ignoring my question.

Now in my fifties, I'd like to be flattered that this younger woman is paying attention to me, but I know what this is...she's not flirting with me. She genuinely thinks she's met me before and is trying to figure out where or how.

"So, Morgan, why do I feel like I know you?" Olivia asks.

"I don't know," I respond. "But it happens to me a lot."

"That's weird...what do you mean?"

"Parties, airports, restaurants, bank lines, all sorts of people," I attempt to explain. "I catch people staring at me, and I can tell what they're thinking at that moment. They think they know me. Some people say something, others just try not to stare."

"Are you secretly famous or something?" she says, flashing an even bigger smile.

"Not that I know of," I say. "In fact, once people start talking to me and realize they probably don't really know me, they often become visibly uncomfortable. Either that or they open up to me about their lives, then feel uncomfortable the next time they see me."

"Funny you're saying that," she says. "I was thinking about how I told you all about my family during our pool lessons, and I'm not sure why. It does feel a bit awkward around you now...like you know our secrets and you really shouldn't."

"Wish I knew what to tell you. But I've never really been able to figure out what this is...this familiarity thing. Truthfully, I can't say I like it. I think the familiarity ends up pushing people away in the end. You should have seen the way your dad left the table, started to come back, then quickly ran out the door and up to the sun deck. That was him not wanting to talk to me anymore, not about an urgent need for a suntan."

"Yeah, I suppose that's true," Olivia says.

Olivia shifts her gaze from me to the window behind me. The warmth I was feeling from her intense stare wafts into the air. She looks down at the water droplets left on the table from my cup and begins to trace them with her finger. *Why do I have these conversations?* I ask myself. I always say too much and make people feel uncomfortable. Olivia excuses herself and joins her dad. I assume Jason has made good on his decision to take a nap below deck. I pull out a book and reread the same paragraph three times. My brain feels like it's in overdrive, whizzing from thought to thought.

Here's the problem—I believe that if God talks to me, then he talks to everyone. Most people seem to disagree. I believe this because God (or whatever people would like to call it) has talked to me my entire life, and I'm no one special. I don't believe it's an audible voice that other people can hear, but it's as clear to me as talking to a physical person. I also know it is ridiculous, and it often disagrees with what I'm being told by what I would consider religious people. The voice doesn't sound particularly almighty...it sounds more like a friend who's trying to explain what's going on around me because

I just don't seem to be getting it. There was a period of about ten years after college when I decided to ignore the voice and pretend I didn't hear it. I found that alcohol did a decent job of drowning it out. But, hungover the next day, the voice would return. I finally gave up trying to ignore it at thirty. I know what I hear, and it somehow sounds different from my own inner monologue. It tells me things that will happen or how people are feeling or what I should be doing. When I say out loud what the voice is saying to me inside, it often gets accredited to me as some sort of sage wisdom. But it never feels like something I've thought up. It always feels like it's coming from outside of me. I often don't want to know all these things. Instead of feeling instructional, the voice creates a confusing clutter in my head. If it is God, as I suspect, it seems to me that the voice would come as a comfort. It never does. I also know that all of this is weird to other people. Whenever it comes up in conversation, especially if I say it's God, I hear one of two responses: Either God doesn't exist and you're imagining things, or God does exist, but I don't hear him or her or whatever like you do.

I don't subscribe to either of those views. My version is...I hear God, I'm pretty sure you do too, and, like you, I don't want to follow what I hear because I have my own agenda. Of those who actually believe I am hearing God's voice, their only question then is, "Why wouldn't you want to follow it?"

My answer? I don't know for sure, but maybe I will someday. The neatly packaged religious explanation of God's words leading to peaceful pastures somehow just doesn't ring true for me. Instead, this voice is radically outside of my comfort zone. It scares me. It always seems to be calling me to become something or someone that I do not feel qualified to be. And all of this flies in the face of my modern culture telling me to "just be your true, authentic self." What if working to be my authentic self is getting in the way of what I could become?

As I sit alone at this small table in a boat somewhere off the Kona coast, the voice comes to me saying, "Transformation always begins in the secret place of prayer. I want you to go even further. I know it seems like you've gone a long way, but I want you to go even further... there is so much more. Let go of your preconceived ideas and just follow me."

To Mark, this was nonsense..."bullshit," as he put it. Yet here he was, trying to enter the sport of scuba diving way outside of his comfort zone. Why was he pushing himself to take this journey? Clearly, it was difficult for him. Why not just stay home?

I see him climbing back down the ladder from the sun deck and making his way through the chairs in the galley toward me.

"Listen...I didn't mean to make fun of you earlier," Mark says, leaning against a chair at the table next to mine. "I thought about what I said about how thinking you hear God is somehow weak-minded. You seem like you really believe that stuff...and maybe there was a time I believed it too. I used to go to church. I think Olivia already told you that. I had friends back then and church leaders who said the same thing, just follow the voice of God. No matter how hard I tried, I can't say I ever really heard anyone or anything. I always just felt like my decisions were my own and God didn't really care much what I did, so long as I was a good person."

"So, do you feel like you've been a good person?" I ask.

"Yes," he answers as he flips the chair around and straddles it backward. "I mean, I always tried to be. Sure, I've made mistakes, just like everyone else, but I know a lot of people who are worse than me."

"By the way...you never told me what 'that thing' was," I say, changing the subject.

"What thing?" he asks. I realize I just tipped Olivia's hand. *She* told me about it, not him. I wait to see if that dawns on him. I try to pass it off as if it was he who had told me.

"I don't know. You told me earlier that something happened to you when you were ten years old."

"Oh...*that* thing."

Mark pauses and stares off into space. I wait and say nothing.

"I was out on a frozen lake in Michigan with my brother," he starts, looking over his shoulder to see if anyone else is listening. "I grew up there, and we used to go out on the lakes near our house to fish in the winter. We'd pull our little hut out there, drill a hole in the ice, and sit out there fishing until we were either frozen or caught our limit. We went out early that winter. We should have known the ice was too thin, but we figured we'd be OK. Halfway across the lake, I heard a crack, then I saw ice starting to separate under my feet. Next thing I know, I'm underwater with the hut on top of me. Water that cold really takes your breath away, you know. Somehow, I got out from underneath the sinking hut, but I had drifted away from the opening I cracked in the ice. I found myself looking up through the frozen water at my younger brother, who was trying to get to me. The ice cracked again, and he was next to me underwater. We both surfaced and struggled to get out, but the edge of the ice kept breaking off, and we fell over and over again back into the water. I thought we'd both had it when our neighbor, this older guy who we never talked to much, appeared above us. He reached down and pulled both of us out of the water one by one...my brother first, then me. He had laid one of those extension ladders from the back of his truck across the ice and was kneeling on it so he wouldn't fall through too. He took us home, and our mother warmed us back up."

He stops talking. He's staring at a ceiling light, and I wonder if he's reimagining the whole event in his mind.

"Do you think about that when you go in the water?" I ask.

"Every time we go under the water on one of our dives, I look back up at the surface, and I can see that ice...it's like it happened yesterday."

"Do you think that's affecting your learning to dive?"

"Probably...I just think about how cold it was...how I couldn't catch my breath, even after we got back to the surface. I feel like there's a ceiling above me when I'm underwater...like I'm trapped under there somehow."

To me, being underwater is the ultimate freedom. To Mark, it is a coffin. I have no idea what to say to him on this topic, so I go back to our earlier conversation.

"You may not hear complete sentences like I hear, but God is speaking to you constantly," I say, breaking the silence. "That's the other half of what I mean by prayer, but I sometimes forget to mention it. God is touching your emotions or imprinting images on your mind or putting songs in your heart or people in your life. God is speaking to you right now...what is he saying?"

"See, that's the stuff that makes me uncomfortable," Mark says. "Look, I like you OK. You've been very patient with me, but I just can't relate to you when you start doing that...that...*God* thing."

"I get it," I say. "I know it's weird, but I also believe it's true. I think it's the reason you're on this dive boat with me. And I also think it's the reason I'm sitting here alone in the galley. It's too much for people, but I know it's true. In fact, I think you already heard the voice...something in you wants to listen. Something in you is longing for a new journey. I guess the real question is...will you continue?"

Mark looks at me as if he wants to ask another question. His expression changes, and I get the feeling he's had enough of this for now.

"I'm beat," I say to him. "I'm gonna go catch a nap in my bunk. I'll catch up with you at dinner to talk about tomorrow's dive plans. Enjoy the rest of your day."

"OK," is all he says.

As I'm walking away toward my bunk, I hear, "Transformation always begins within you before it can manifest outside of you."

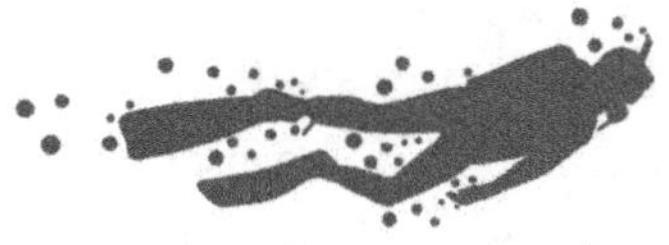

3

The sun rises to the east of our boat on day two, casting an indefinable light across the tables in the galley area. I never woke up from my nap late yesterday afternoon and missed dinner. I awoke in my bunk before dawn this morning, got dressed, and have been reading for hours alone in the salon. I decide to step out to the stern, where a few others are sipping coffee and some are having a morning smoke. Smoking never made sense to me, especially among people who take part in a sport that is all about breathing. How much time have I spent talking about breathing in my years of teaching scuba? Diving really does come down to breathing. Breathing in to supply oxygen to the lungs, which transfers to the blood and fuels the body. Breathing out to expel other unused gases—mostly nitrogen—and the carbon dioxide building up in the lungs and airways as a byproduct.

Mark joins me on the stern, breaking my train of thought.

"Morning," he mumbles over the top of a steaming cup of coffee. "Missed you at dinner last night."

"Good morning," I respond. "Yeah, I guess I was beat. Did you sleep OK?"

He takes a swallow. "Not really," he says. He has a contemplative look about him, as if he's deciding whether or not to tell me what's on his mind. I wait and stare off at a sport fishing boat passing slowly in the distance.

"I just keep thinking about yesterday," he finally says. "I feel like everything is going OK, and I'm doing just fine following you around underwater. Then you ask me to do that damned mask removal and replacement thing, and, I don't know, it just starts this panicky feeling in me. Then I have trouble getting the water out, which leads to an even more panicky feeling...then it's like I just lose control and the next thing I know I'm at the surface."

"You're not exhaling," I say.

"What's that?" he asks.

"You're not exhaling," I repeat.

"Yeah, I heard you. I just don't know what you mean by *I'm not exhaling*," he says. "I'm talking about clearing my mask."

"I know about the mask. What I mean is that panicky feeling comes from not exhaling."

I've explained this a couple of times to Mark, and I'm debating whether or not I want to explain it again. I decide to take the plunge.

"When you don't fully exhale, you trap carbon dioxide in your lungs," I say. "More and more carbon dioxide builds up and signals your body to breathe more rapidly. But rapid breathing builds up even more carbon dioxide. It's a vicious cycle. Try holding your breath, and you'll notice when you get to the point you can no longer hold your breath, you want to exhale, not inhale."

"I don't understand what that has to do with panic," he interrupts.

"Your body wants to get rid of the carbon dioxide, but you're holding it in because deep down, you don't think you're going to get another breath since humans can't breathe underwater," I say. "That creates a feeling of urgency in your body, like you need to do something fast or you're not going to be OK. Holding your breath also deprives the reasoning part of your brain, the prefrontal cortex, of oxygen, which also feeds that panicky feeling. As the prefrontal cortex shuts down, the decision-making process gets pushed over to the instinctive side of your brain, or the limbic lobe, where emotional behaviors, like panic, reside. Your instincts serve you well on land, but they can get you into big trouble underwater with scuba. Your instincts are telling you to hold your breath, but you must learn to fully exhale while scuba diving to control your breathing. If you can learn to control your breathing, you can learn to control that panicky feeling. The feeling may never completely go away, but you can control it."

Seems simple enough, I'm thinking as I explain the process once again to Mark. But students naturally start holding their breath underwater. Their bodies take in air just fine, but they don't want to exhale because they know instinctively, like Mark, they can't breathe underwater, so they tend to hold their breath, which makes them feel like they can't breathe, pushing them to full-blown panic.

"We're going to take a dive today with no skills," I say to him. "You and I are just going to take a fun dive and work on your breathing. I really believe if we can get your breathing—well, mostly exhaling—under control, it will solve most of your problems."

He nods but says nothing. He seems to be thinking about what I just said, but I'm not convinced he believes me. On my suggestion, we go back inside the galley area and slowly move through the buffet line of scrambled eggs, bacon, potatoes, toast, bagels, and various condiments. We sit down with Olivia and Jason, who are already eating. I remind them they're certified Open Water Divers now, so they can plan their own dives for the day. I tell them I'm going to be diving with their dad this morning to work through a few things and I'll rejoin them this afternoon. Mark has enough dives under his belt to complete the course, but we can't seem to get past this mask removal issue. He can clear a little bit of water out of his mask, but he can't meet the requirement to completely remove the mask from his head, put it back on his face, and clear it without losing his mind and bolting for the surface.

As we eat a quiet breakfast, I gaze out the window across the turquoise water in the bay where we are moored for the day. It is cool in the air-conditioned galley. Warm, tropical air is circulating outside, fogging the edges of the windows. This is a beautiful location along the Kona coast on the Big Island of Hawaii. I've traveled to many beautiful locations over the past twenty-five years to teach this sport I love, and I've been diving decades longer. I couldn't wait to begin scuba diving as a teen, signing up for a course a month after my fifteenth birthday. The courses were tougher back then, with ex-Navy diver instructors seemingly trying to talk students into quitting. But the courses have become much friendlier over the years, opening the sport to a wider cross-section of humanity all the way down to the age of ten. Warm water, cold water, clear water, murky water—I've taught in many settings. But no matter the location, the problems are the same, and they always start with the inability to exhale.

As we sit in silence, I become aware of the small waves gently nudging the hull of the boat. The waves remind me of the voice... always there but only noticed in stillness. The voice is the oxygen that feeds my soul but is so easily drowned out by the poisonous carbon dioxide of negative thoughts toward myself and other people that I allow to build up in my head. The volume of the voice is always dictated by how I'm doing in relationship to others in my life and how I feel about myself. The voice whispers to me, "Transformation enters when unforgiveness and bitterness exit." The times I am unable to forgive people or forgive myself build up thoughts and feelings inside my brain. The thoughts of these soured relationships and negative self-images then spiral out of control and consume my thoughts. I know the only way to clear the thoughts from my head is to forgive the person who I believe had wronged me or maybe even to forgive myself, but I am unable to do so…just like Mark's inability to exhale. Something gets held inside me that allows nothing else to enter. How do I get Mark to exhale?

There is so much swirling in my head, I forget I'm sitting at the table with three other people. Olivia and Jason quietly stand and clear their plates from the table, depositing them on the galley counter before making their way to the dive deck. I sit silently with Mark as we peer out of the doorway and watch them pull on their wetsuits, don their gear, and begin to dutifully go through a pre-dive safety check to prepare for their dive.

"You ready to give this another try?" I ask, turning my face back toward Mark.

"Um…yeah, sure," he says, returning my gaze. He's staring intently into my eyes as if looking for something to boost his confidence. He follows me to the dive deck, where I instruct him to put on his wetsuit as I wriggle into mine. Zipped into our suits, we assemble the rest of our gear and sit down on the bench in order to slip into the BC shoulder straps on our kits. He watches as I pull my mask strap over my head and let my mask dangle under my chin. He duplicates my actions and turns to locate his fins a crew member has placed on the bench beside us.

"Like I said, no skills on this dive," I say. "We're just going to have a relaxing dive and focus on our breathing. As the captain told us, the bottom off of the stern is about 100 feet deep, but the mooring buoy the boat is tied to on the bow is anchored at forty feet. So, we're going to jump in off the stern, then swim around to the bow and follow the mooring line to the bottom." I give him the rest of the run-down regarding hand signals, air consumption, safety stops, and the general plan.

"Sounds good," Mark says. "So…what do you mean by focusing on our breathing?"

"You may not remember from the pool sessions," I respond, "but I talked about a long, slow exhale like this…" I take in a deep breath, then start exhaling, counting the seconds out on my fingers… one, two, three, four, five, six, seven, eight, nine, ten. "I want you to breathe in so deeply you can feel the waist strap on your BC getting tight. Then I want you to breathe out and count your exhale on your fingers."

He takes a deep breath, then exhales to count five.

"Deeper," I say. "Try it again but take a deeper breath." He begins to inhale. "Keep going, keep going, keep going." He continues to inhale until it is obvious he can't inhale anymore. "Good," I say. "Now exhale slowly while counting to ten on your fingers." He does. "Good. Now try it again with your mask on and breathing through your regulator."

He self-consciously looks back and forth as another group of six divers on board starts glancing over to see what we're doing. They, like Mark, are also learning to dive. Their instructor, Carlos Mendes, dutifully watches as his students finish assembling their gear. Carlos, who's probably twenty years younger than me, looks at Mark, then glares at me. I assume from his glance he is questioning my ability to teach this student. Based on my observations of him on the boat and the prior week on the beach, my teaching style differs from Carlos's style. He's one of those instructors who talks too much and gives too many instructions. There's no way his students can remember everything he says. I'm betting he thinks I don't give enough instruction.

Mark looks back at me and dutifully puts his regulator in his mouth. He takes in a deep breath, then quickly exhales.

"No, that's not it. Try again. Deeper inhale…now count the exhale on your fingers."

He finishes the exercise then spits his regulator out.

"Do you trust me?" I ask.

"I guess," he responds. "I mean, I trust you enough to be out here scuba diving with you off a boat in the middle of the ocean."

"Do you trust me that I know what I'm talking about?" I continue. "Do you believe me when I say I've seen this in hundreds of divers over the years I've been teaching scuba? Do you trust yourself that you can do this?"

I look away from Mark and quicky scan the dive deck. Carlos, his students, and all of the other groups of divers on the boat, including Olivia and Jason, have jumped into the water and started their dives. One of the four deck crew members, Nate, slowly makes his way toward where we are sitting. Nate is tall with dark, curly hair framing his deeply tanned face. His bare feet at the end of long, thin legs move gracefully over the deck. Mark is looking down at his own feet and doesn't notice Nate, who now has a quizzical look on his face as if asking if we're OK. He stops about ten feet from us and looks directly at me. I flash him an OK sign with my hand. He smiles at me and turns on his heels to head back to the swim step, where the rest of the deck crew is standing and keeping an eye on the divers' bubbles percolating to the surface of the calm water.

"Mark," I say, breaking the silence. "I know you can do this, but *you* have to know you can do this. I'll keep trying with you as long as you want to keep trying, but I can't really make you do anything."

His eyes have become a darker shade of red, and he's starting to tear up. He doesn't strike me as the type of guy who cries very often, especially around other men. But I've seen odd, emotional moments play out before with other students. I once had a diver begin sobbing and collapse into a lounge chair beside a swimming pool as I was prepping her to simply jump into the water. Something about the act of learning to dive taps into all sorts of pent-up feelings. I put my hand on Mark's shoulder as he wipes his eyes and tries to catch his breath.

"I don't know why she did it," he says.

"I'm...I'm not really sure what you're talking about," I say.

"Kate, my ex-wife...I'm not sure why she cheated on me," he says. He stares at the horizon as if he's watching the movie that is his life.

"What the hell?" I say to no one. I'm not sure what to say to Mark. He is trembling. His hands cover his face. Tears seep through his fingers and begin to drip from his chin.

"With my best friend too," he chokes out between sobs. "At least I thought he was my best friend till he started sleeping with my wife... son of a bitch. I kept a good job, loved my kids, helped out around the house...I don't know why she did it."

Mark and I are sitting alone in the Hawaiian sun, baking in our wetsuits, and gently rocking back and forth with the swells. A bead of sweat trickles down my spine.

"I'm happy to get out of this gear, go inside, and just talk if you want to," I say.

The curtains close on the movie seemingly playing in his mind, and the lights come on in his eyes. He wipes the remaining tears from his face and looks at me. I feel an emotional connection to him, as if I've somehow been invited into the depths of his life. I hear, "Just *be* with him...there is nothing to say." He appears to be debating how much more he's willing to let me in. I don't get the feeling he talks much about this part of his life, and, frankly, we've only known each other for a couple of weeks.

"No...no," he says, shaking his head. "I want to make this dive."

He wipes his face again with the back of his left hand, and we stand up together. We lumber over to the starboard side of the boat where we'll make our "giant stride" entry into the water. Nate quickly hops up the two steps from the swim step back onto the deck to assist with our entry. We will enter the ocean through a small gate in the rail, dropping about three feet into the water. The swim step is reserved for divers exiting the water. I see Nate check the valve handle on Mark's tank to be sure his air is fully turned on. A pre-dive safety check, masks in place, regulators in our mouths, a little air in the BCs to make sure we float, fins on our feet, and over the side we go. The water is seventy-nine degrees, as it has been all week. It is a welcome shock to my system in contrast to the warm sweat in my wetsuit from sitting on the deck. The water in Hawaii is often cooler than most people think, especially in the winter. People who have spent much time in the Caribbean or the Gulf of Mexico think tropical waters should be eighty-five degrees. Every once in a while, Hawaiian waters get into that range, but currents around the islands typically keep it in the high seventies. The cooler water has a reviving effect as we plunge off the boat.

I look over at Mark as we bob at the surface. An odd expression sweeps over his face. He seems more relaxed than I have seen him on this entire trip. The edges of his lips begin to curl, but he stops himself from breaking into a full-blown smile. I assume he would still be upset after talking about his ex-wife, but his eyes are bright as he looks at me through his mask.

We swim toward the bow of the boat and grab a hold of the mooring line, which is gently moving in the small, smooth swells. I look across the surface of the water and innately know this will be a good dive. I don't know why exactly; it's just a feeling that comes over me from time to time. The weather is perfect. I plunge my face into the water and look down through my mask. I can clearly see the reef sixty feet below us and the mooring line angling off into the shallows. Mark looks down, then back at me. He gives me the OK sign when I point my thumb downward to signal our descent. We slowly make our way down the line toward the bottom. He stops to pinch his nose through the mask skirt and clear the pressure from his ears. We continue to descend. We pass Jason and Olivia as they are ascending up the line to end their dive. We exchange OK signs, and my mind registers how long Mark and I must have been sitting on the boat talking as I notice most of the other divers making their way back to the surface.

We drop off the line near the bottom at forty feet, and I find a sandy spot to touch down. Typically, I try to keep my students off the bottom, as it's not great for their gear or the tiny organisms living in and around the reef. But I want Mark to feel relaxed by gentle contact with the open patch of sand below us. Our fin tips lightly touch down. I get Mark's attention and signal to him that I want him to watch me. As he watches, I take a deep breath from my regulator and start exhaling while counting on my fingers...one...two...three... four...five...six...seven... eight...nine...ten. I motion with my hands open, palms up, as if offering him a gift, to let him know I'd like him to give it a try. He takes a long inhale and exhales to a count of six. I open my hands again, palms up, and flip my left hand over onto my right, as if turning back the pages of a book, to let him know I want him to try it again. On his second try, he makes it to eight. I clap my hands slowly in mock applause to show my approval. I motion for him to follow me.

We both put a small burst of air into our BCs, and we slowly rise up off the sand to swim over the reef. Various types of coral pass beneath us in an array of colors. The neon blue, yellow, and red hues of the fish swirling around us and the abundance of life creeping over the reef have a hypnotic effect as we slowly kick along, careful not to touch the delicate coral. The reef gives way to another long patch of sand, and I can see where it picks up again about twenty feet away.

I motion to Mark to follow me across the sand to the other section of reef. I stop Mark about halfway to the next section of reef and hover about three feet over the sandy bottom. I take a long breath off my regulator and exhale to a count of ten on my fingers. Mark does the same, this time making it all the way to ten. I give him a fist bump and continue swimming. He folds his arms gently across his chest as we swim and takes long, slow kicks. He looks remarkably different from his other dives when he was making short, irregular kicks and flailing with his hands to keep his body correctly trimmed in a horizontal position.

After thirty-seven minutes of cruising the reef, we return to where we started at the bottom of the mooring line. I had told him we would not be doing any skills on this dive, but I get the feeling he may be able to remove and replace his mask. I scrawl with a stubby pencil on my underwater slate to ask him if he is up for trying this skill again. He nods his head and gives me an OK signal but then points at me. I infer from his pointing that he wants me to do it first.

I typically only demonstrate diving skills during the swimming pool portion of the course, but I figure Mark could use the encouragement by watching me. I motion for him to watch me as I take my mask completely off my head. I continue breathing through my regulator, careful not to inhale through my nose, which is now exposed to the water. After a few seconds, I replace my mask, take a deep breath through my mouth, press gently against the top of my mask, and exhale through my nose, forcing the water out the bottom of my mask. I point to him to let him know it's his turn. He signals OK to me. I watch him closely—the moment of truth—this is when he usually panics.

I move in close to him, stare into his eyes in an attempt to impart confidence and gently clutch one of the straps dangling from his vest. Mark removes his mask and strap from his head and holds it with a firm grip. He breathes easily through his mouth into the regulator without getting water up his nose. I can't believe I'm watching this…I can't believe he's the same guy who shot to the surface yesterday.

He slips his mask back onto his face and stretches the strap around his head. He hesitates to catch his breath, then he takes a deep inhale through his mouth and exhales a long breath through his nose to clear his mask. His mask is completely free of water as his eyes blink open. I'm elated...I don't know what to do. I inadvertently smile, breaking the mouth seal on my regulator and nearly inhale some sea water. I can tell he is as surprised as I am. Another fist bump. I would embrace him if I thought I could get my arms around all of his gear. We both float, staring into each other's eyes. The moment feels spiritual, as if something has broken free in Mark.

I hear again, "Just *be* with him." Neither of us move. We simply float about two feet apart, staring at each other. I look away first, breaking the spell. I motion for him to follow me, and we slowly make our way back up the mooring line, making a safety stop at fifteen feet to allow a bit of the nitrogen built up in our bodies to work its way out of our bloodstream through our lungs.

Once at the surface, we swim back to the stern of the boat. Mark deftly removes his fins and hands them one-by-one to a waiting crew member while holding onto the ladder. I notice a smile etched into his face. His climb back onto the boat is steady and smooth. I follow him up the ladder and over to the benches where we remove our gear. Mark can't stop smiling. He doesn't appear to be the same guy who sat with me weeping over his failed marriage about an hour ago. Nate walks over to check on us.

"How'd it go down there?" he asks.

"Fantastic. A beautiful day for diving." I answer. I then say loudly enough for others on the dive deck to hear, "Oh, and we have our most newly certified diver sitting next to me."

"Congrats!" Nate says, offering a high five to Mark. A small applause and a couple of cheers erupt from the divers and crew milling about. Olivia emerges from the salon and walks over to where we're sitting on the bench.

"Well?" she asks.

"He did it!" I say to her.

"We knew you could do it!" she says, leaning in to give her father a kiss on the cheek.

Mark looks around the deck at the other divers and crew, who are all smiling and looking his way. He raises his hand as if to say thank you, then stares down at his feet.

He tilts his head to the side to look at me and says, "Thanks for sticking it out with me. That breathing thing really works. It makes a big difference."

"You are more than welcome," I say. "Just happy to see you made it through the open water certification."

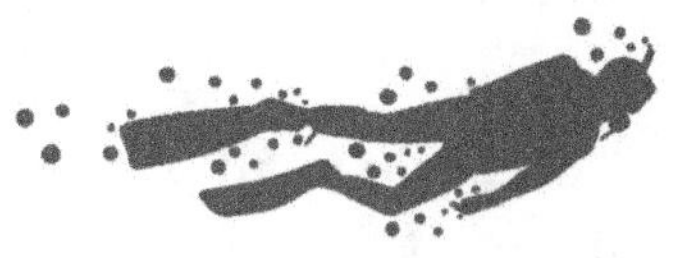

4

Something happened to Mark earlier that day when he broke down about his failed marriage. I think back to how Olivia had told me her parents always seemed to be fighting. She was glad to leave home for college at eighteen, she had told me, to get away from the "negative atmosphere." She spoke of her father as an involved parent who always seemed interested in what his children were doing. But when it came to her mom, he just never seemed to know what he was doing—he didn't even know how to talk to her from what Olivia had said. And despite her portrayal of Mark as a good parent, I also got the feeling from something in the tone of her voice that he may not have been the most devoted father either.

I've heard this story from many men throughout my life. They tell me how they have kept a steady job and brought home a paycheck...how they never cheated on their wives and tried to help around the house...how they really felt like they were trying hard. They also tell me how their wives just don't seem to fully appreciate any of those things and want more.

Mark's story was similar, and he tells me more about it after dinner as we sit together in the galley area. Olivia and Jason have already finished their dinners and are on the other side of the salon playing cards with Carlos and one of his students. I look across at their little group. They're chatting as they play cards. I'm annoyed with Carlos and have been avoiding him.

The previous week, during the first open water dive off the beach with Mark, Olivia, and Jason, I was conducting a buoyancy check. One at a time, I had them place their regulators in their mouths then completely let the air out of their vests. Holding their breath, they should float about eye level in the water. When they let that breath out, they should slowly sink. I had them in fairly shallow water so they couldn't get far if they began to sink and forgot to reinflate their vests. I also held their tank valves behind their back as they performed the exercise one-by-one, just in case I needed to gently tug them back to the surface.

I give my students freedom to make mistakes. I'm there to stop anything truly dangerous from happening, but I'm not there to correct every little mistake step-by-step. I purposely let them make minor mistakes, then debrief them later to let them tell me what they think went wrong and how they could improve next time. I've found this to be a more effective way to learn. If I never let them make mistakes, they just become more and more dependent on me instead of learning how to fix problems themselves. Not all instructors share this view.

As I conducted the buoyancy check that day, Olivia appeared to be weighted properly, Jason was bobbing like a cork, and Mark was sinking like a rock. As usual, Mark was struggling the most, and I let him struggle. I had a hold of his valve but was letting him sink to see if he would reinflate his vest of his own volition. He had a grip on his low-pressure inflator hose, but he was not pressing the inflator button to add air to his BC. Instead, he was kicking wildly to remain at the surface.

We were diving at Puako Beach, a popular dive and training spot on the Big Island. Carlos was meeting his students at the same beach, but they had not yet arrived. Carlos taught scuba full-time for a local dive shop and seemed to view me as an intruder, as I teach mostly private lessons part-time and affiliate with many shops in many locations.

He was surveying the site from the rocks on the beach and noticed us in the water. He began yelling at Mark to put some air in his vest. I looked over at Carlos and yelled back that the situation was under control, but he continued to yell at Mark to inflate his vest. After a few minutes of struggle, Mark turned toward me, spit out his regulator, and began climbing on top of me, which is a typical reaction of someone who thinks they are about to drown.

I could see the panic in Mark's eyes as he pushed me underwater while attempting to crawl on top of me. I slipped my regulator into my mouth so I could easily breathe. I knew Mark was safe, and I knew I could escape his grasp by sinking deeper under the water. Drowning victims will always let go if they feel you sinking underneath them. The last place they want to be is underwater.

Once Mark released his grip on me, I swam up behind him, reached over his shoulder, grabbed his low-pressure inflator valve, and inflated his vest for him. I eventually got him to calm down, and later that day we walked through all the steps of a buoyancy check and what went wrong. The situation in the moment looked life-threatening to anyone looking on, but it was actually under control and became a teachable moment.

"That seemed kinda dangerous what you were doing out there," Carlos later told me between dives back on the beach.

"It was a simple buoyancy exercise," I replied. "I had it under control."

"Didn't look like it," he said.

"I'll tell you what," I said. "You teach your students and I'll teach mine."

As I packed the rest of my gear away and closed the tailgate on my rental pickup truck, I overheard him tell one of his students I was "dangerous." I think I also heard him tell another student as they walked off to do their second dive of the day that I was an "asshole."

His first comment was incorrect, but his second comment had an element of truth. I decided I didn't like him much after that day and sensed the feeling was mutual. We also didn't really appreciate each other's teaching styles. He thought I was neglectful, and I thought he was overbearing...that was my summation of our relationship. After that, we would watch each other with a critical eye.

Sitting at the table that evening, I wondered if my relationship to Carlos would have been different if we'd encountered each other under different circumstances. The truth is that no two instructors teach in exactly the same way. We teach the same materials but have very different ways of communicating with students.

Some take a militaristic approach, some take a step-by-step approach, while others take more of a self-discovery approach. I had never really fallen into the drill sergeant school of teaching, but I was certainly step-by-step early on in my instructional career. I was communicating every step in detail with my students when I started out, until one day I noticed another instructor with the same approach. I watched as he went on and on about every single detail of their next dive and all of the associated skills they would be performing and all of the potential problems to avoid. It was thorough, but it was too much information...a lecture instead of a conversation.

I watched as his students' eyes glazed over, and I wondered what they were thinking. I figured from other experiences they were probably mostly wondering if they were going to get cold in the water, or if they put enough time on their parking meter, or maybe even if they could die underwater. They were not really hearing anything he was saying.

I noticed the same look on my students' faces in my next class. I vowed that day to keep my lectures much shorter and ask my students more questions to keep them engaged. And, instead of expecting perfect adherence to all of my instructions, I learned to expect mistakes.

The primary objective is always to return safely from every dive, so I take steps to ensure the mistakes are kept from becoming dangerous situations. But creating teachable moments from mistakes is part of the process of learning to dive. I began to notice I was turning out more competent divers at the end of my courses who had actual problem-solving skills.

I remember wanting to share my discovery with other instructors I knew, but most of them were not very receptive to this idea. I could never figure out why until one day it dawned on me that the method I had chosen was way harder and more time-consuming. I actually had to get to know my students and tailor my teaching style to each of them individually. To do this would require me to cut down my class sizes.

Dive instructor standards allowed me to take up to eight students, conditions permitting, into the open water with me, and I could do so in a safe manner. But the allowable eight was often too many for me to give individualized instruction the way I wanted to in many cases. I started dividing those groups into two smaller groups for each dive, when I deemed it necessary, which meant twice as many dives for me for the same amount of pay. The financial incentive to divide into smaller groups did not exist, especially in high-volume dive centers, so most instructors were not willing to go that route.

We're still sitting at the dining table in the salon when Mark begins to notice I'm staring at the group playing cards on the other side of the cabin. He snaps his fingers to get my attention.

"What's up?" I ask, turning back toward him.

"I just didn't know what she wanted," he says to me.

"You just didn't know who wanted what?" I ask.

"My ex...I didn't know what she wanted."

"Maybe she just wanted you," I respond. I'm surprised when I realize he wants to continue the conversation from his breakdown on the dive deck this morning.

"She had me," he says. "I was crazy about her."

"Maybe she didn't know it," I respond. "Maybe you were doing all those things to please her but never really gave yourself to her."

Mark sets down the soda can he just opened and is now staring at me as if this is all making sense somehow, but he doesn't know why.

"Men, myself included, struggle with this idea," I continue. "We think we're doing what our wives or girlfriends want us to do, but we're not communicating well. My wife wants to partner in what I'm doing, and she wants me to partner in what she's doing. She's far more interested in what I'm doing *with* her than me telling her about what I'm doing *without* her."

"Yeah, but I had to go to work to support the family," he says. "I couldn't be with her all the time."

"I'm certain she knew that," I reply. "But when you were with her, were you really all there? I mean, were you really present, or was your brain somewhere else? Were you glancing down at your phone while she was talking? Were you thinking about what she was saying or were you somewhere else in your head, thinking about work the next day or the game you were missing on TV while you were talking to her? I find that women are typically more perceptive than men... they know when you're really present or not."

"Yeah, I mean, I guess I know what you're saying, but I couldn't listen that attentively all of the time," he says.

"Maybe she found someone else who would," I respond.

"So, you're saying she cheated on me because my former best friend Jack listened to her better than I did?" he asks in a disdainful tone. "I don't know about that...seems like a poor excuse."

"I'm sure it was much more complicated than that," I say. "But I'm also sure that had a lot to do with it."

"Who knows," he says. "But this is making my head hurt, and I'm gonna go to bed." He leaves the table and heads off to his bunk.

Sitting alone, I think about how one of the biggest blocks to hearing the voice is unforgiveness and bitterness. People tell me all the time they never hear "God's voice" like I do. But as I probe a bit deeper, I can always find some unforgiveness toward another person. In Mark's case, it is clearly his ex-wife. I hoped he would eventually find a way to forgive her in the sense that his failed marriage would not forever be at the forefront of his thoughts.

The way he would talk about his marriage always left me with the feeling he knew he had something to do with its failure. I believed he knew that he had disengaged long before his wife cheated on him, and, in a deeper sense, he was having trouble forgiving himself...the side of unforgiveness that really messes most people up.

I sometimes catch myself saying things like, "I should know better by now" or "I always do that" when I mess up. Sitting there, I began to realize that these pronouncements I make are actually forms of unforgiveness toward myself. No wonder forgiving other people is so hard. I can't forgive others because I can't forgive myself...I can't give away what I don't have.

I had listened as Mark fretted about not being able to complete his mask-clearing skill while "everyone else in class" was able to do it. He couldn't step outside of himself for a minute to see what was going on. He was convincing himself that he could never do it. The feeling he was holding onto about his lack of ability was physically causing him to hold onto his breath.

On the aft deck this morning, he shed many tears for his ex-wife and himself and their failed marriage. In a moment of breakthrough, sitting on that sun-drenched bench, he started the process of forgiving her and forgiving himself…the beginning of letting himself move on. The proof happened underwater when he was finally able to fully exhale, breathe deeply, and focus on the task at hand.

The transformation he sought was to move from fear back to a place of boldness, the very trait that had attracted Kate to him in the first place. Whether or not his marriage could ever be salvaged (he told me she was no longer with Jack) was for another day, but he had to start his life over with a step of forgiveness. The relationship they shared had died, but maybe they would be able to resurrect something new.

I decide I'm ready for bed as well. I clear my remaining dishes and head down to the bunks.

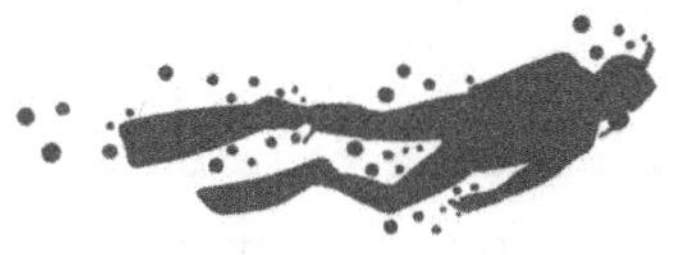

5

Day three dawns on our boat, and I turn Mark loose with his new certification to dive with Olivia and Jason. After breakfast, I watch as they gather on the dive deck and assemble their equipment with freshly filled tanks. They go through their pre-dive safety check, make their way to the side of the boat, slip their fins on, and plunge into the water. They slowly swim toward the bow and make their descent.

This morning, I would be diving alone. Diving certification agencies do not generally recommend diving alone. We teach people to adhere to the buddy system and stick close to their buddies for safety. Truth be told, most of the people I dive with are still learning and a far bigger liability to me than an asset. These student divers would not be able to rescue me in an emergency and were far more likely to get me *into* trouble than *out* of it. I had also learned and taught others over the years to be self-reliant divers, which is a diving certification unto itself. I carried redundant breathing systems and had volumes of practice with emergency surfacing techniques. Above all, I had learned to calm the panic that can overcome a diver in stressful situations.

That being said, this is a hotly debated topic within the scuba industry, and the statistics regarding diver fatalities don't support the idea that buddies, regardless of their ability, are a greater risk than an asset.

I follow all of the procedures to set up and put on my gear, go through my mental checklist, and commit myself to the ocean with a giant stride through the gate in the starboard railing. I look back at the boat to signal to the divemaster on duty that I'm OK and see divers putting together their scuba kits and making plans for their dives. I turn toward the east, where the sun begins a lazy ascent into the sky.

Another beautiful day off the Kona coast—calm, clear, and warm with fluffy clouds making their way across the horizon. I don't know if the tourists notice it, but there is a distinct spirit to Hawaii, and I can feel it strongly today. The spirit there is not a sense of religion...it goes far deeper and is entirely personal. There is something palpable in the air I can feel the moment I step off the airplane.

Each of the islands carries the spirit, but it was somehow stronger to me on the Big Island. I take a moment and let the feeling wash over me as I bob at the surface. The feeling is even stronger for me in the water, and I'm about to enter my sanctuary.

After decades of diving, I've never grown tired of it. Every dive feels like a new adventure to me. For some reason, I just can't get enough of it. At the same time, I never made it my true profession. Yes, I'm paid to teach others to scuba dive, but I avoid fully immersing myself into the industry.

I worked in a dive shop long enough to know the retail side of the business is not for me. I have nothing against the equipment side of the industry, I am just not interested in selling gear. I also teach enough to know that working at a dive resort fulltime or running a dive boat is not for me either.

For me, diving is a spiritual exercise that has to be balanced with the rest of my life. I have done many things over the years—writing for newspapers, working in tech, and now owning my own small businesses—but diving is always reserved for certain times and places. It is sacred to me. From the time I was baptized in a small Michigan church by my grandfather to my last dive, the water remains a way of cleansing away the past and starting anew. I had burned out on many activities and jobs, but I tended to my diving activities like a secret garden. I'm always careful to do just the "right amount" of diving and instructing.

I begin my descent along the anchor line, passing a few divers on the way. Midway down the line, I let go and begin a lazy, free descent to the bottom at about eighty feet. I shoot a puff of air into my BC and make my way along the reef to the west and into deeper water. I level off at a hundred feet deep for a portion of my dive, then swim over a drop-off to 130 feet, the recreational diving limit.

I'm diving with oxygen-enriched air, known as nitrox, which will allow me to remain at depth longer. The science of diving with oxygen-enriched air holds that by reducing the amount of nitrogen in the breathing mixture, a diver can remain at depth longer by not amassing so much nitrogen in their bloodstream. This works well to extend dives but creates a secondary concern over oxygen toxicity leading to convulsions if diving too deep...a classic case of too much of a good thing.

I'm attentive to remain above my maximum operating depth of 132 feet for my gas mixture, but I also let my mind go to the solitude of the deep. I tell my students that true diving starts at one hundred feet deep. At shallower depths, monitoring your air supply is the primary activity. After a hundred feet, the added concern of no-decompression limits from breathing compressed air becomes much more uncompromising.

Due to the surrounding pressure, each breath in the deep contains far more molecules of oxygen and nitrogen that will need to be processed through the bloodstream. The oxygen is burned off by the body, but the nitrogen remains intact on its way through the pulmonary system. Breathe the heavy mixture at depth too long and there is so much nitrogen in the blood that you cannot simply return to the surface.

Divers exceeding those limits expose themselves to decompression sickness (the bends), where the nitrogen begins to bubble in the bloodstream as the diver returns to the surface. Those bubbles expand in the arteries and veins as the diver continues to ascend to the point where they block blood flow. This condition causes pain and numbness in the diver's extremities and can cause complications in the heart, lungs, and brain, leading to death in serious cases. The remedy is to stay within the designated times at various depths, as indicated on my diving computer.

Thinking about such physiological complications while diving comes in complete contrast to the simple beauty of the bright orange cup coral firmly attached to the reef and a multitude of crimson fans waving gently in the glow of my dive light. I turn my head and spot a sea turtle slowly swimming up behind me. I can see and hear rainbow-colored parrot fish nibbling away on the coral. I feel as though I belong here. But too much time on the reef and the fact that I'm an invader into this space will become readily apparent.

I look away from the reef into the deep blue void and see the shadow of something large moving toward me. The sea turtle has ducked behind the reef, and a dark shape the size of an old Volkswagen bus comes into focus. I squint to get a better look and see the telltale dark spots and stripes of a tiger shark.

The tiger shark is a formidable predator in these waters, and she looks to be at least fifteen feet long. The Hawaiian name for the tiger shark, niuhi, simply means a "man-eating shark," and the tiger is considered one of the more dangerous to humans. She is by far the biggest shark I've ever seen up close, and she is clearly aware of me. But instead of fearing this man-eater, I'm transfixed. I can't take my eyes off her. She is beauty and grace as she slowly glides through the water.

At the same time, I know she is capable of tremendous bursts of speed and vicious attacks. I know what she can do to me. I also do not think we are somehow spiritually connected, as some do, and she means me no harm. Instead, we share a mutual curiosity and cautiousness toward each other, as if we both want to know what the other is doing here on the reef.

The spell breaks, and I become very aware this is her domain and not mine. She passes by me then makes a big turn and heads back my way. Tiger sharks are considered to be sacred *'aumākua* (ancestor spirits) by native Hawaiians. Maybe so, but I am a *haole* (non-native Hawaiian), and this shark is not related to me. I'm completely vulnerable, and she gets to decide what happens next.

I remain still, thinking about my breathing, which has accelerated. I catch my breath and consciously slow it down by focusing on my exhale...one...two...three... She heads toward me, passing so closely I feel I could reach out and touch her. I fight the urge to extend my hand. Touching her is not a great idea for either of us, despite what some divers say. My hand moves slightly, and she adjusts her trajectory as if she knows exactly how far she is from me. I watch her dark, lifeless eyes drift by. She continues on her way and passes back into the blue. I glance down at my wrist-mounted dive computer and notice I only have three more minutes at this depth, so I decide to start heading back up the reef into shallower water.

As I swim, I think about the tiger shark and how much of my life is beyond my control. I have the choice to place myself in certain circumstances. I can choose to be on the reef or just stay home. But often the outcome of my choice involves a variable, the shark, making it impossible to think I'm ultimately the one in control. The process of transformation is the same.

I am transformed by events in my life, but the process starts with me. I respond to the call or "prayer" I hear in my soul, and the journey of transformation begins. This response brings up old wounds in my heart, and a process of forgiveness must start or I stop. Once forgiveness works its way through my life, I find myself at the place of fasting, which is just a fancy way of saying giving something up that has become dear to me, voluntarily or not.

I surface near the mooring line and return to the stern of the boat, where I remove my fins and climb up the dive ladder.

"How was your dive, John?" Nate asks in his typically cheerful tone.

"Fantastic," I respond. "Saw a massive tiger off the edge of the reef."

"Oh, you must have seen Nina," he says with a smile.

Somehow, knowing this shark has a name creates a familiarity in my mind that downplays her potential ferociousness. A lie many divers would like to believe at depth.

"You guys named her?" I ask.

"One of the captains who used to run this boat named her Nina," he responds. "No one seems to know the whole story since it happened like twenty years ago…you know tigers can live about fifty years in the wild. The version of the story I've heard is that he was attacked by a young tiger shark off this reef. He was spearfishing, and she was interested in the fish on his stringer. She moved in to take a bite of his fish and took a chunk of his leg in the same bite. I guess he lost a lot of blood and ended up in the hospital for several days."

I sit down on the bench and slowly work my way out of my gear. There are no other divers on the aft deck. I assume everyone else is still in the water or inside eating lunch. Nate appears to be done with his story, but I want to know more.

"So, where did the name Nina come from?" I ask. I'm thinking about Columbus's famous ships, the *Niña*, the *Pinta*, and the *Santa Maria*. *Niña*, pronounced *Neen-ya*, meaning girl in Spanish, was often mispronounced *Nee-nah*.

"I heard the name Nina…I think he actually pronounced it *Nine-ah*…came from niuhi, the Hawaiian word for tiger shark," Nate said. "I don't know, Hawaiians have a lot of stories for a lot of things. They don't seem particularly bothered that one story can have many different origins or meanings…you kind of get to pick your own meaning."

Nate's story clears up absolutely nothing in my mind, but it does get me thinking about how different people have different interpretations of the exact same events. I walk back into the galley area and decide to skip lunch, although I grab some fruit on my way past. Breakfast had been big that morning. I check in with Mark, Olivia, and Jason, who are sitting at our regular table. I tell them I'll catch up with them after lunch. I head down to the bunk room where I plan to take a nap.

I lay down in my bunk, but my mind is swirling…I'm lost in thought, and my life starts playing over in my mind. I'm taken to a place five years ago that I don't like to visit. I was eating Hawaiian food nowhere near Hawaii when I got the worst phone call of my life. I stepped out of the restaurant in the San Francisco Bay Area, where I was eating with my wife Mary, to take the call from what my caller ID said was the US Coast Guard. I knew my sons were out fishing that day near Catalina Island, about thirty miles off the coast of Los Angeles, and I immediately knew something was terribly wrong. *Please, God, let them be arrested for something stupid*, I thought as I answered the phone. *Please let them be sitting safely in a jail somewhere*, I said to myself. I heard the Coast Guard officer say my youngest son's name, James. "Please God, please God…no," I muttered under my breath.

The officer slowly explained to me that there had been an "accident," and both of my sons wound up in the water. My older son, Ben, had managed to get back on the boat and radio for help. He was injured, but in stable condition in the little hospital on the island. My younger son had not been found. The Coast Guard had begun a search, but the officer had little information. I hung up and dropped to my knees.

The Coast Guard and sheriff's department would search for days. He would never be found. My life and my family were dramatically and forever changed.

The details of that day and the effect it has had on Ben, who tried to rescue his twenty-three-year-old younger brother, will forever play out in my mind. The boat was small and not very stable. A step in the wrong direction and the vessel would lean far to the side. On a clear and calm summer day, the boat tipped too far while under way, and they were both thrown into the water.

James had been born with a genetic condition that caused a substantial curvature in his spine and also would not allow him to fully extend his arms and legs. Despite several life-threatening surgeries to correct his condition, his spinal curvature left him with forty percent of what would be considered normal lung capacity. I know from teaching scuba that much of human buoyancy comes from the ability to fully inflate your lungs. James loved the water and hated life vests, which left him not very buoyant and struggling to stay afloat.

Ben worked hard to save him that day, even heroically diving down and bringing him back to the surface, but the end had already come. Somehow, Ben managed to get ahold of the boat as it circled back, but he was drawn under its keel and into the outboard propeller. He lost sight of his younger brother as the propeller wrapped up his pants and cut deeply into his leg. His pant leg material wrapped so tightly around the propeller that it thankfully stalled the motor, allowing him to slowly work his way free and climb back on the boat to radio for help. A passing fishing boat came to his aid, and ultimately the Coast Guard responded.

Laying there in my bunk, I can see Mary's face in utter confusion as I tell her the news. I can hear her weeping in the middle of the night for her lost son. The grief still cuts deeply into both of our lives and often makes it impossible for us to *be there* for each other. I wouldn't say I became suicidal, but I do remember thinking for years that if I didn't wake up the next morning, that would be OK with me. The pain was and is too much to bear.

Mary began to dream of bringing her life to an end, attempting to shoot herself but botching it and leaving me with an invalid wife to take care of. She dreamed of jumping from the Golden Gate bridge, only to have the hood of her sweatshirt catch on a bolt, leaving her dangling and waiting for the fire department to pull her back onto the bridge. Yes, we still had Ben, his older sister Meridith, and a grandchild to live for, but that still didn't seem like enough to keep on living.

The movie in my head stops, and I drift off to sleep. I awake thirty minutes later with a Bible verse in my head that I had memorized as a child in Sunday school ...

I have learned to be content whatever the circumstances. I know what it is to be in need, and I know what it is to have plenty. I have learned the secret of being content in any and every situation, whether well fed or hungry, whether living in plenty or in want. I can do all this through Him who gives me strength.

I don't understand the meaning of any of this, so I close my eyes again...I can see James's face and hear his voice calling out to me as he sinks into the abyss. How can I ever be content with life again since losing my son? I know I am not the only one to have suffered great loss, but that doesn't matter to me right now. I am adrift in my own world, knowing others still depend on me to continue in this life, but wondering if I even care anymore. I had learned much about myself and grown in ways I could never have imagined since losing my son. I even saw an aspect of God I had never seen before. But knowing those things, I still would never have voluntarily made that exchange for the life of my son.

"Transformation includes appetite management," the voice tells me.

What is that supposed to mean? I ask. *Are you asking me to fast... give up my son...sacrifice more to be transformed?* There is no response to my question.

I had built businesses, I had raised children, I had remained in a committed relationship with Mary for decades, and I knew that life required sacrifice. Every great story I had ever heard, watched, or read always contained a sacrifice. But I was not interested in my life becoming a great story. I was not willing to make the sacrifice. Is this what the spiritual discipline of fasting was all about? Fasting is a part of every world religion, but why do people purposely deprive themselves of food or something else they love (and maybe even need) to learn some spiritual lesson? Was fasting somehow practice for the inevitable loss that comes with life? Loss is certain, and my ability to somehow manage it is the determining factor as to whether or not I would be able to keep moving forward in a way that resembled a contented life.

This process of transformation I had been learning and teaching for years always starts in a place that feels like the desire of the heart. It starts with some sort of longing. Moving through the stage of forgiveness and letting go of bitterness was always the next step. Forgiveness always feels like letting go...it always feels like loss in a way, but the next step would be the real loss.

But fasting as practice for dealing with loss? Too much to comprehend. The loss had dropped into my life like a tiger shark emerging from the blue. It was there to take something from me that could never be replaced. I had voluntarily given up small things in my past for better choices...a comfortable seat in front of the TV in exchange for exercise at the gym, the warm embrace of alcohol for sober awareness of my pain, walking away from the table while my stomach was not yet full.

In a way, fasting may have been a practice for the losses to come that would be beyond my control. But it had not prepared me sufficiently for the loss I would experience. I managed to find the strength to continue in this life, but the desire was gone. True loss is meat being stripped from the bone. It feels unsurvivable. It is permanent. It leaves you walking with a limp. And after years of limping, I had finally gotten to a place where every conversation did not include a description of the loss of James. But the story was still always playing out in the back of my mind like a computer program running in the background. The loss was sucking away resources needed to run the primary functions of my life.

I force my eyes open, roll to my side, and emerge from my bunk to make my way back to the galley area. Mark is now sitting alone trying to figure out his dive computer.

"I can't figure out how to get my dives off this friggin' computer," he says as I sit next to him.

"Here, let me see it," I say. I walk him through the steps to look through the logs on his computer that keep track of all the dives he has made. "Did you have a good dive with Jason and Olivia?"

"Yeah, it was awesome," he says, beaming. "I can't believe I finally made it through my certification."

"I knew you would," I say, patting him on the shoulder. "It takes time."

"It didn't for Olivia and Jason," he snorts.

"We all get stuck at different places," I say. "It doesn't really mean much, other than we're all different and carry our own baggage."

The conversation meanders through trivial matters—the weather, baseball, dive computers—and back around to Mark's divorce.

"I've been thinking about some stuff you said to me," he says.

"What kind of stuff?" I ask.

"You know, stuff about me not being very...*present* was the word I think you used."

"That was the word," I say.

"That was probably true," he says. "But it's not really an excuse for her cheating on me."

"I never met your wife, so I don't really know much about your situation."

"I felt like we had a good marriage. I mean, we argued and stuff, but I never thought we'd split up," he says. "Looking back now, it almost seems like it was inevitable. We had definitely drifted apart, but I thought we'd eventually drift back in the same direction. Then I got to thinking about how much of my life just felt like drifting. After she left, I decided to try and be more intentional about my life. That's part of the reason I signed up for diving. My kids kept asking me to try it with them, and last month I finally thought, what the hell...why not? Now I'm sitting here feeling like I've forgiven her in a way. That should make me feel better, but I feel worse."

"Do you feel like your marriage can still be saved?" I ask.

"Not a chance," he says flatly. "Not a chance, brother. I think that's what is bothering me now. I feel like I'm coming to terms with the fact that it's over and will never be again. I feel like part of my soul got ripped out, and letting myself experience that pain almost seems necessary for me to move on."

"You've started grieving," I say.

He looks at me and starts to speak. He catches himself and looks past me out onto the dive deck.

"Yeah, I guess that's it…maybe," he says finally. "I've been so angry at her that I never grieved the loss of our marriage…funny, I never really thought of it that way."

Mark slowly stands up, gives me a little nod, and heads off to his bunk for his afternoon nap. Loss is the theme for the day. I had seen the tiger shark face-to-face, although no other divers I had spoken to reported seeing her. Even Nate, who told me her name, had never seen her in his years on the boat. Nevertheless, she was out there, cruising the reef, staying just out of sight from all of the divers but me. She is always looking for opportunities to take away. She may have spared us all harm that day, but life had not.

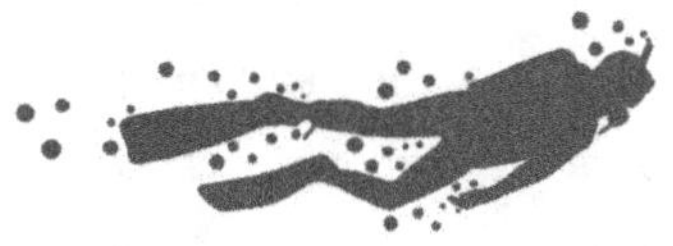

6

I sit straight up in my bunk, nearly hitting my head on the bunk above me. We are not in staterooms, as is the case on more expensive charter dive boats. The *Hibi'o* instead has a shared space below deck with rows of semi-private bunks stacked two high. The bunks are relatively comfortable, but this is by no means a luxury charter.

Most of the time, I don't remember my dreams, but this one was so vivid that I got up and wrote it down. In the dream, I was staying at a hotel attached to an airport. I was in an elevator descending to the sidewalk below. At the curb, I was to catch a shuttle bus to the airline terminal. The elevator was a tangled mass of luggage and people. As the doors opened on the street level, the crowd surged forward, pushing me out of the elevator. I began wheeling my roll-aboard bag with my right hand toward the shuttle bus while carrying my computer bag in my left. As I stepped onto the bus, the driver told me he was going to take a break, and the bus wouldn't be leaving for another fifteen minutes. I climbed back off the bus and began to contemplate my options.

I knew I didn't have much time to make it to my flight. I wasn't far from the terminal and decided walking would be faster than waiting for the driver. At the same time, something was telling me to go back and check the elevator one more time because I had left something behind. I walked back to the elevator and pressed the button. The doors slowly opened, and I saw an old garment bag hanging against the wall of the otherwise empty elevator. I remembered carrying this bag years before switching to a much more convenient roll-aboard bag in my business travels. But for some unknown reason, I knew the old garment bag held the things I needed for this particular trip. I also somehow knew it had been packed by my wife Mary and not me. I reached out to grab the bag and found myself sitting in my bunk wide awake as dawn broke on day four.

I lay back down on my bed, pondering the meaning of this dream. I pull out a small journal I keep in my bunk and begin writing down what I had seen. As I'm furiously writing, I can hear the voice clearly saying, "The thing you think is an inconvenience will be the thing that causes you to go back for the thing you really need...pay attention."

Wait...what? That doesn't make any sense, as usual. Why does this voice I can't seem to shut off speak in riddles? The voice is clear, but it doesn't make sense. "Think...think," I say out loud. If I had not gone back for the garment bag in my dream, I would not have what I needed for the trip. It was inconvenient to go back and get it out of the elevator, and my delay may have caused me to miss my flight.

So...were the contents of the bag somehow more important than the flight itself? Did I think I was being inconvenienced, when maybe I was never intended to get on that flight? And how did I know Mary had packed that bag? Did she have something for me that I was forgetting?

"Hey...you going to join us for breakfast?" Mark asks, interrupting my thoughts. He is standing near my bunk with only a dark curtain separating us.

"Um, yeah...in a few minutes," I respond. "Just waking up." I realize most everyone else is already awake and moving about the bunk room.

I'm typically awake before most of the passengers, and I can tell Mark thinks it's odd I'm still in my bunk. I smell bacon cooking in the galley area above. There is nothing that smells as good as bacon cooking in the morning, so I lie down again to take in the aroma and let myself just be in the moment.

What do I consider an inconvenience, and what is the thing I really need? These must be the right questions because the answer begins to crystallize in my mind.

I often forget what feels like an *old garment bag* of self-development and preparation of those around me when I race to get to the *flight* of a new project or business or activity. I rush to get started, rush to get out the door, and rush through the preliminaries because I want to get to the good part faster. But in so doing, I often leave things—or, more important, people—behind. I don't like lingering in the place of development...I want to get the real thing underway as soon as possible. My American culture has taught me to be impatient, to want the future now...lost is the idea that my goals will be reached over time through patience and in community with others.

I hold strongly to the conviction that my job on this planet is to be part of building something bigger than me that will last and benefit others way beyond my lifetime. To do that requires me to patiently lay a proper foundation for generations who will come after me. But instead, I find myself thinking so much about my needs today that I stop thinking about what future generations will need from me tomorrow. I've also lost the patient practice of saving for the future and, instead, borrow money to get what I want now. But in so doing, I'm borrowing against the future instead of building toward the future. Tomorrow is never better because I've already spent it today.

Like a bookend to my thoughts, I hear again, "The thing you think is an inconvenience will be the thing that causes you to go back for the thing you really need."

Mary naturally thinks generationally. She thinks about her children and her grandchildren. She holds something I do not. I *know* things in the spiritual sense of the word. I understand there is much more going on in my life than what meets the eye, but I misunderstand how to translate that to a life I'm still living. She instinctively knows how to live that out while still on earth.

I open the curtain and climb off my bunk. A quick trip to the head to brush my teeth and I'm back in the galley area. I move through the buffet line and gather my breakfast of bacon, eggs, and coffee, choosing to skip the potatoes. I sit with Mark, Olivia, and Jason, who are already eating.

"I've never seen you sleep in," Olivia says with a wink. How is she perpetually in a good mood? I can't help but smile back at her.

"Yeah...well...I had this weird dream, and I wanted to write it down so I wouldn't forget it," I say.

"Do tell," she says.

I relay my dream to the three of them between bites. There's no response, so I continue to describe my analysis of what took place.

"Sounds like what you said to us in our dive class," Olivia says. Jason and Mark are not really listening. They're talking about Mark's dive computer.

"What do you mean?" I ask her.

"Well, you kept telling us to *trust the process* and take one step at a time," she responds. "You told us not to get overwhelmed looking at the big picture or trying to jump ahead, but instead just concentrate on the next skill or step. Sounds like you're not following your own advice. So, this dream of yours...what are you going to do about it?"

"I don't understand," I say, plunging my fork into the scrambled eggs on my plate.

"So, what's the next step?" she asks. She pauses to sip her coffee. "What's the inconvenience you don't want to deal with...what's the thing you have to go back for?"

I remember her telling me she has a PhD in psychology. I can hear the therapist talking to her patient.

"I'm not sure," I say. She smiles again and says nothing. She stares at me. She leans in closer. Her eyes squint as a quizzical look sweeps across her face.

"I'm thinking about something I used to teach back when I was a *church guy*," I finally say to her. "I used to teach people about personal finances."

"Back when you were a *church guy*." She says *church guy* slowly, as if I've said the words with such disdain that she can taste my bitterness. She is very perceptive. I never talked to her about being a *church guy*. I realize she overheard me one night on the boat when I was talking to Mark about being raised by church-going parents and being very involved in a local church later in life.

In fact, I had studied theology in college and always thought I'd serve as a pastor, like my grandfather, in a church later in life. That never happened, but I raised my own children in a church. Now I found myself *way* outside of the church. I thought people in church were well-meaning, but I was losing the connection between what Jesus taught and the church life I was living. The *business* of church also never made any sense to me. I thought of Jesus as a way of life, not as a non-profit organization with some sort of spiritual hierarchy. Maybe the organization worked for some people, but I could no longer make it work for me. I'm sinking rapidly into the rabbit hole of my thoughts when she stops me.

"Sorry about the *church guy* thing," she says. "Although I am curious what made you leave the church...but some other time...what were you saying about personal finances?"

"People would ask me all the time how God could be *good* if he wouldn't even provide them enough money to cover their needs," I respond. "'If I just had more money,' they'd say, 'I wouldn't have these problems.' Bear in mind, these were not people who were starving by any means. My answer was always the same, 'Lack of money isn't your problem...taking care of the little money you do have is the problem. You're begging God for more money, but why would God supply you more money when he knows the burden that comes with more money would crush you? What if God is trying to build up strength and discipline in you with small amounts of money so you can carry the weight of bigger money to come? You're so busy complaining about lack or squandering the little bit you have or borrowing to get it now that you're missing the very lesson you need to carry the blessing that is to come. What if money is the problem, or more accurately the *test*, and not the solution?'"

"You sound like a preacher," she says. Her mouth breaks into an even bigger smile, and she is openly laughing. "You crack me up. You say dark things like you're *way outside* of the church, but you talk like you're still in it."

"No, I don't," I say a bit too defensively. "Well...maybe I do...I mean, I agree with many of the principles taught in church, I just don't understand the organizational part."

"Kinda sounds like you got hurt by someone and you're blaming the whole church for it," she says.

"Could be," I say somewhat dismissively. "But just to finish on the personal finance thing...I would teach that financial discipline or *stewardship* is an 'inner' discipline. Stewardship is learning to always live within my means and save for the future, either mine or my children's or my grandchildren's. The discipline starts in my brain by denying the desire for immediate gratification. Once the battle for the inner discipline of stewardship is won, I can better see the outer victory of financial increase. The increase becomes an effective tool for building, not just a bigger pile of money and stuff for me now but building a legacy. My inner victory leads to outer victory."

"Kind of like what you were saying to my dad about controlling his breathing," Jason says. I'm stunned as I turn to look at Jason. He never volunteers any information, and when I ask him a question, he never gives me anything but one-word answers. I didn't even think he was listening to my conversation with Olivia, who also turns her head to look at Jason. Mark raises an eyebrow as he looks up from his meal. He drops his fork, and it clatters on his plate. He tries to recover it and knocks it onto the floor. Jason ignores the fork that Olivia is now also trying to recover from under the table and keeps talking.

"You know what you were saying about getting his breathing under control and how it would make solving his other problems underwater much easier?" he continues. "I noticed that was true for me also. Look...I know you don't think I'm listening. I just don't like yapping all the time like you guys do. And this inner victory thing sounds kinda new-agey to me, but it sorta makes sense. It seems like if you can fix the problem in your head first, it makes fixing the physical problem outside of your head a lot easier."

We are all now staring at him. No one says anything. He stops talking and sips his coffee.

"Well said," I say, not wanting to add anything. After a few more minutes of silent eating, I ask, "So, are you guys interested in starting your advanced open water certification?"

We have three and a half more days on the boat and plenty of time to complete the dives that would comprise their next level of certification. There were five dives needed: three dives from the dozens of PADI specialties available, plus an underwater navigation dive and a deep dive somewhere between sixty and 100 feet.

"I am," Olivia says.

"I'm in," Jason says.

We all look at Mark.

"Yes," Mark says with some hesitation. He then points his thumb in the general direction of Jason and Olivia. "But I want to make one more dive with these two this morning before we start. OK with you?"

"OK with me," I say. "Over lunch, we'll review those chapters I had you read in your advanced book and make our first dive this afternoon."

"Sounds like a plan," Olivia says.

The three of them stand up and drop their dishes off with the galley crew on their way out to the dive deck. I watch through the aft doorway as they plan their dive and wriggle into their gear. They stand, make their way to the side gate of the boat, put their fins on, and jump into the water one by one. They are clearly getting more comfortable with each entry.

I now understand Mark's hesitancy when we spoke about the advanced certification at breakfast...diving deeper into the unknown. He had gotten comfortable with their relatively shallow dives. The seventy-five-plus feet of visibility had been spectacular. The weather was also cooperating, with calm seas and a gentle breeze out of the east. The light rain came each evening, but not until the diving had concluded for the day and we were inside eating dinner. We would gaze at rainbows every evening on the western horizon as the sun was setting. But today would be different for Mark. There was more development to take place as we ventured into deeper waters, and I would also ask them to contemplate a night dive.

We reconvene around the lunch table and they, mostly Olivia, talk about all the life they had seen on their dive. A pod of dolphins had moved into the area and were curiously inspecting the divers. I had been freediving with just a mask, fins, and a snorkel that morning, mostly just to interact with the dolphins near the surface. Dolphins universally elicit joy in humans. When there are dolphins in the water, people want to be in the water with them. When there are sharks in the water, very few people want to be in the water with them. They are both fascinating creatures, but they stir up very different feelings...adoration versus dread. Transformation requires both. Fear and joy are asked to dance together as people move through one phase of their life to the next.

"So, I thought he was going to take my mask off my face," Olivia says, concluding a story I wasn't really listening to. "Are you listening?"

"Um, yes...well, no...I was thinking about something," I say in response, realizing I hadn't heard anything she said.

"The dolphin," she repeats, "He was so close with his mouth open, I thought he was going to pull my mask off. Those suckers got a lot of teeth when you look up close."

"Were you scared?" I ask.

"Not really," she responds. "You just feel safe around dolphins for some reason."

I'd read about various dolphin attacks on humans but decide not to cite them to her. They are large, powerful, and wild creatures that can seriously damage and easily kill a person in the water. While there have been reports of such attacks, people just can't get enough of them, me included. There is some sort of natural bond most people feel with them in the water that is difficult to explain. Yes, they get a lot of good press, but there is a feeling that goes beyond just good public relations when you see them in the wild, a feeling that contrasts sharply with the emotion I felt with the tiger shark I saw yesterday. Sharks have always fascinated me, but I don't typically swim toward them when we cross each other's paths underwater.

"Let's talk about your advanced open water dives," I finally say, snapping myself out of my daydreams. Lunch is fish tacos. And once again, the chef on this trip has outdone herself.

"Do we really have to do a night dive?" Mark asks. The fear of the unknown creeps back into his voice.

"No, it's no longer a required dive for the advanced certification like it used to be," I answer. "But Jason and Olivia asked if we could do a night dive, and I highly recommend it. Everything is different at night...a whole new world opens up on the reef. Things you don't see during the day come out at night, and the true-white light from your dive light makes the colors way more vivid than they are during the day."

Mark doesn't look convinced. He says nothing and stares at me like I've lost my mind. Jason and Olivia lean in closer as if they want to hear more about the mystery of night diving.

"I'll tell you what," I say. "Let's get through the first few dives for the advanced certification, then we'll talk about a night dive. They all nod but say nothing. I can tell Mark is still skeptical about the idea.

"So, the first dive is going to be our Peak Performance Buoyancy dive," I say. "We'll be doing a few different exercises to help you get better control over your buoyancy. We want to keep you from accidentally rising to the surface or dragging along the bottom. Once you find that neutral space, I want to teach you how to stay there. In order to do that, once again, you're going to have to control your breathing."

"Why is everyone looking at me?" Mark asks no one in particular.

"Sorry, Dad," Jason says. "We just know you've been struggling with your breathing and we want to see you get better at it."

"Sorry...didn't know I'd become the problem child," Mark replies.

"You're fine," I say. "But I do want to get your breathing a little more dialed in so you can enjoy diving more."

I discuss various weight systems, including weight belts, vest-integrated weight systems, tank weights, and ankle weights. I discuss each system and its pros and cons and relate how every diver's body is not the same and different systems work better for some divers than others. I talk about the various pieces of equipment and how they each affect buoyancy and how steel scuba tanks are less buoyant than aluminum tanks. In addition to the Peak Performance Buoyancy dive, we will also be doing an underwater navigation dive, hopefully a night dive, a deep dive, and a wreck dive. On the navigation dive, they will learn how to better navigate underwater using a compass and how to measure distance along the bottom. The deep dive and the wreck dive will happen when we anchor up in the next location.

We move out to the dive deck and begin getting our gear ready for our first advanced dive. We do our pre-dive safety checks, walk to the rail, slip on our fins, and jump through the gate into the water. This buoyancy dive will be a relatively shallow dive of about eighteen to twenty-five feet. As I explain to them, it's much harder to control your buoyancy near the surface where the most noticeable changes in pressure occur. If they can master buoyancy control in the shallows, they can easily translate those skills to the deep.

Once in the water, we begin a leisurely swim to the anchor line at the bow. We do a final check with each other, and I give the thumbs down sign, indicating we will start our descent. Just before I slip under the water, I notice darker clouds moving in from the eastern horizon. The water is still calm, but I wonder what the conditions will be like when we resurface at the end of the dive. We make our way down the anchor line and settle near a sandy spot at the bottom. I have Jason float in a vertical position with his legs crossed underneath him. I put a little burst of air into his BC until he's floating motionless about a foot off the bottom. I write on my underwater slate that I want him to notice how he rises a bit with each inhale and sinks back down with each exhale. I had explained to them earlier how breathing is integral to buoyancy control and how movement in water always requires anticipation and forethought.

Breathing underwater to control buoyancy is like steering a boat, which is very different from steering a car. To steer a car, you turn the steering wheel in the desired direction. The steering system then angles the front wheels to the right or left and the rear wheels pretty closely follow on that path. When you turn the wheel on a boat, the motor or the rudder in the rear of the boat turns, pushing the stern to one side or another. Because the steering happens at the stern, the boat slides sideways a bit across the water on a turn. This sliding has to be factored into every turn. A boat will not always follow the desired path, and the person steering can easily oversteer, which pushes the boat too far to one side or the other. Add wind, waves, or current to that equation, and it can be difficult to steer a boat in a straight line. To steer a boat straight, you turn the wheel slightly to stay on course, then as the boat begins to respond, you must start turning back slightly in the opposite direction to keep the boat straight. I remember steering my uncle's fifty-foot boat when I was a kid. I would feel like I was steering in a straight line, but when I'd look back at the boat's wake, I could see I was zig-zagging through the water...oversteering. When you're learning to scuba dive, the zig-zagging happens in an up-and-down direction instead of side-to-side. To prevent the up and down, divers need to anticipate each breath. As they feel themselves start to rise on the inhale, they need to already be exhaling to keep themselves at the same depth in the water column. As they feel themselves start to sink on the exhale, they need to already be inhaling.

Jason was close. He inhales and begins to rise, then starts exhaling a second too late and begins to ascend toward the surface. I pull him back down a few times until he starts to get the hang of it. Olivia also catches on quickly, and soon, the two of them are hovering like genies above the white sand. Mark is struggling to maintain his buoyancy. After a dozen or so tries, he relaxes a bit, breathing in and out more deeply. He is beginning to see the effect it is having on his buoyancy. Once the three of them are floating weightlessly in the water column, I motion to Jason to flood his mask and clear it while he continues to float. Many people can get to the place of weightlessness so long as they are concentrating on their breathing. But as soon as I give them something else to think about, like clearing their mask, the buoyancy control goes out the window.

I make them each flood and clear their mask with varying degrees of success. I motion to have them follow me over the reef, working on buoyancy control, then slowly back up the anchor line and back onto the boat. We stow our gear and start a debrief on the buoyancy dive.

"I felt like I was really getting my buoyancy under control until you made me clear my mask," Mark says.

"Yeah, me too," Olivia says. "Why is that?"

"You've been breathing on land for a long time," I respond. "You've been breathing on land so long that you almost never think about it. It's just a reflex action your body knows well...it's not a conscious effort. Like I said before, breathing underwater is a conscious effort because the *way* you breathe makes a big difference. If you breathe in deeply on land, you don't float up off the ground. Buoyancy is not a *normal* thing to think about, so it requires conscious thought. When I had you clear your mask, you started thinking about not breathing through your nose and the steps to clearing and forgot to think about how breathing was affecting your buoyancy. The trick is to practice buoyancy control until it becomes second nature and moves to the reflex portion of your brain. That will free up your conscious mind to think about other things. I have you flood your mask to show you where you are on that learning curve. When breathing and buoyancy control become second nature through repetition, your mind will be free to concentrate on other aspects of diving."

"That's what I was saying before," Jason says. He is quickly becoming our group's resident philosopher. "You know...about fixing the stuff in your head before you can fix the stuff outside of your head."

"Huh?" Olivia says.

"If I want to change my behavior, I have to consciously make an effort over and over again until it becomes something I don't really have to think about," he continues.

The confused look on Olivia's face tells him she still doesn't quite get the point he's trying to make.

"Remember when Dad taught you to ride a bike?" he asks her.

"No...not really," she says.

"You don't ever remember stuff from our childhood," he says. Olivia shrugs off Jason's comment. I wonder if the trauma of emotionally distant parents caused her to block out memories from her childhood.

"C'mon, you have to remember," Jason continues. "He took you out onto that big field at the playground and let you fall a bunch of times until you figured out how to balance. No one can really *teach* you how to balance...you just try over and over again until your body somehow figures it out. You start off consciously thinking about leaning to one side or the other and you usually lean too far and fall over. After lots of practice, you figure out how not to lean so far and you stay upright."

"What does that have to do with breathing underwater?" she asks.

"Think about it," he replies. "Dad told you he would let you ride on the grass so you didn't have to worry or think about falling. The grass would be a soft landing. He also said you wouldn't have to worry about going too fast because the resistance of the grass on the tires would keep you moving slowly. It was brilliant, really."

Mark, the proud papa, is suppressing a smile now. I wonder if he's thinking about his son calling him brilliant or he's just remembering teaching Olivia to ride a bike.

"I mean, think about it," Jason continues. "He was trying to teach you balance by eliminating all of the other distractions. Once you had the balance thing down, he could then take you out on the street to start learning how the brakes on the bike worked…how to speed up and slow down…how to stay out of traffic and a bunch of other stuff."

"So, flooding my mask while still learning to control my buoyancy was kinda like trying to learn how the brakes work on a bike while still learning how to balance?" Mark asks me.

"Not sure I've ever thought of it that way specifically," I respond. "But that makes sense."

I look over at Jason, who is lost in thought, as am I. Even after decades of diving and teaching diving, I'm still learning myself. There is always a better way to teach or make diving relatable. If I keep my mind open to learning, my students teach me as much as I teach them. The transformation process is not just for them. It's for me also.

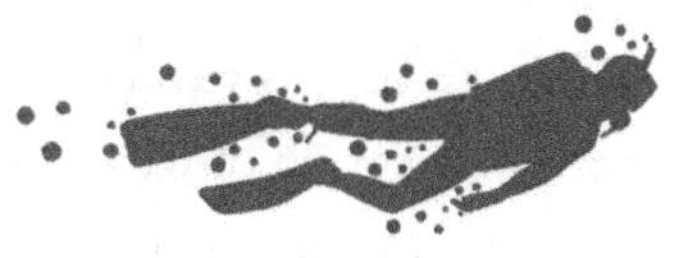

7

The dark skies I had seen earlier sit on the horizon as if deciding whether or not to come any closer. The sun is setting, but there is still plenty of light on the dive deck. I sit with my three students in the galley area, deciding what I should or should not tell them about our night dive. If you're sane, the idea of submerging yourself into inky black water at night is a bit unnerving. I'm not sure of the exact number, but I've done dozens of night dives. Even so, there is still a bit of hesitation before I jump off a boat at night—nothing I admit openly to my students. They don't need to know what I'm feeling right before jumping in…they have enough on their minds already.

"I thought you said we'd do a few more advanced dives before the night dive?" Mark asks me.

"I did, but changing conditions can alter the plans," I reply. "The captain said the conditions may get worse, so he couldn't guarantee any night dives after tonight." Mark appears satisfied by my answer, but still nervous about the idea of a night dive.

"It can be a bit disorienting when you first jump off a dive boat at night," I say to Mark, Olivia, and Jason. "But you'll get used to it pretty quick."

How far do I want to get into the primal fear of darkness most humans carry deep within them? We are naturally creatures of the day and not well equipped to function at night in the wild without technological help. I've explained this to students in the past with mixed results. For some, a description of what they are about to experience helps them prepare...for others, it adds to their growing anxiety about committing to the dive. I split the difference with this little group and give some explanation without going into too much detail. I also decide not to tell them the story of the harbor seal in California's Monterey Bay.

I was leading a group of advanced students there one evening. We were doing a relaxed shore dive near the breakwater jetty at San Carlos Beach, a popular training spot. The conditions were calm, and it was a beautiful night with a full moon. Despite having to don cold, clammy wetsuits—still wet from our dives earlier that day—all the divers were in good spirits and ready to go. We entered the water slowly, turned on our dive lights, and began a slow underwater swim along the jetty. There is a very narrow range of vision on a night dive...just the width of your flashlight beam. Visibility was good that night, and we had a relaxing swim along the rocks of the breakwater, passing numerous bright-purple sunflower sea stars and a curious octopus extending a tentacle toward my light.

Imagining what might be swimming just outside of your flashlight beam on a night dive doesn't take much creativity. Great white sharks inhabit the waters of every ocean in the world, but there is a concentration of them off the northern coast of California. Everyone who enters those waters knows there are great whites around and has seen the videos of kayaks being nibbled on or heard the stories of surfers being thrust into the air by big sharks rising from the depths. On the other hand, there are less threatening, yet fascinating, creatures that become much more active at night: lobster, octopus, eel.

As we swam along the Monterey breakwater, I remembered Palancar Reef off the tiny island of Cozumel in Mexico. During a night dive there, I saw the reef come alive at night with thousands of brightly colored sea snakes. There were so many snakes, the reef itself seemed to be undulating. My thoughts of the warm Gulf Stream pushing me along Palancar were jolted back into the cold water of Monterey as a large, mostly-white animal jetted in front of me. A great white was my immediate thought as I recoiled and nearly dropped my flashlight. Whatever it was swimming through my field of vision left me feeling defenseless and panicky. None of the students following me had seen the white blur, and I had to resist the urge to bolt to the surface. As my brain caught up to the adrenaline pushing through my veins, I realized it was a white harbor seal that had nearly swum into me after I startled it with my light.

Fortunately, I remembered the answer to nearly every problem underwater is "just breathe."

"So, what happens if my light shuts off during the dive?" Mark asks me, drawing my attention back to tonight's dive.

"That's why you have a backup light," Jason interjects.

"Besides, we all have flashlights," Olivia adds, "and those little light stick thingies we put on our tanks."

Mark listens to his children but doesn't look convinced.

"I mean…I guess…I'll give this a try," Mark says. "Just not sure this night diving thing is for me."

"This whole trip was your idea," Olivia says. "And you knew we wanted to do a night dive."

"Look, we'll just take our time and move slowly along a relatively shallow reef," I interject. "Besides, there's nothing out there at night that isn't out there during the day. The darkness just boosts your imagination."

"I heard sharks feed at night," Mark responds.

"They can sometimes be more active at night, but sharks are more opportunistic than anything else," I say. "They're looking for an easy meal...an injured fish, a weak-swimming creature. If you watch them, you'll notice they don't just swim around indiscriminately eating everything in their path. They swim around looking for opportunities."

"Enough shark talk," Olivia says. "Everyone's gearing up already. Let's get out there."

The four of us walk out of the salon back to the dive deck and start checking our gear. Everyone experiences fear at various times. I'm certain Olivia and Jason feel the same anxiety that I feel and Mark feels...well...maybe Mark feels it a bit more in this instant.

While ridding yourself of fear entirely isn't really possible, learning to manage it can go a long way. Fear can also be useful, keeping you alert to potential dangers around you. But letting it make your decisions is where the trouble begins.

We ready our gear at the edge of the boat and once again plunge into the ocean. Jumping into the ocean at night is hard to describe. There's a split second when you step off the boat where you simply have to trust you are prepared and everything will be OK. There's an innate fear when humans go underwater, and that feeling is amplified at night. But there is a calm that also comes with being underwater at night—a feeling of surrender to the ocean—a surrender that lies just beyond fear.

As I watch my students adjust to the elements and begin to explore the reef, I realize much of their ability to overcome the natural fear of the ocean at night is trust in me that I won't put them in a situation in which they will be in true danger. I will not present them with a problem I don't think they can resolve. I'm glad they trust me, but do they also trust themselves?

We had decided beforehand that Jason would lead this dive, and, so far, he is doing an admirable job. He gathers us near the anchor line and signals a descent with a thumbs-down motion. We obediently deflate our BCs and follow him down the line. I'm transitioning them to diving more without an instructor and, instead, building more confidence to continue leading their own dives. There will be other students to teach, and this part of the trio's journey with me will end soon.

Jason turns to see if we are following him and shines his dive light on his hand to give us the OK signal. We each shine our light on our own hand and signal OK back in response. I'm impressed that everyone remembered not to shine their lights into each other's eyes, as many do on their first night dive. We look back at the reef, and it has come alive under our lights. During the day, most of the color of the reef is absorbed by the depths, leaving everything in shades of blue. But at night, under artificial white light, vivid red corals, bright orange sponges, and neon-yellow tangs on the reef take on extra brilliance.

The dive continues at a relaxed pace. I tug on Jason's fin to remind him to stop so we can experience my favorite part of a night dive. I regain control of the group momentarily and signal to each of the divers to turn off their lights. One by one they shut off their lights, and we're left in the dim red and green light of the glowsticks attached to our tank valves. I wave my hand through the water, and sparks of multi-colored phosphorescent plankton swirl from my fingertips. The other divers follow suit, and we're soon surrounded in phosphorescent light. I notice a larger shape moving just outside of our circle and make out the tip of a manta ray's fin. Mantas are often attracted to divers' lights in this part of Hawaii. The light activates plankton, the manta's favorite food. I turn my light back on as the eight-foot span of the manta's wings slowly brushes over my head. I see the telltale spots on the manta's belly that are unique to each animal. Regular divers off the Kona coast can actually identify the individual mantas by their spot patterns.

As the manta swims off, Jason regains our attention by waving his light and signals with his hand to ask each of us how much air we have remaining. He makes the decision to turn back toward the boat and signals us with a circling motion of his light above his head. As he motions, I detect the presence of something else that is large and moving around our little circle. I don't know if I can actually see a shadow or I just *sense* there's something circling us in the same way you can feel it when someone's staring at you...even from behind. Mark turns, quickly shining his light away from our little group. His beam catches the tail of a whitetip shark as it angles away from us. He immediately looks back at me, moves closer, and shines his light in my face. I'm blinded temporarily and push his light away. I shine my light between us so we can just make out each other's eyes in our masks. I find myself again trying to somehow impart confidence and calm into Mark with a simple stare. I can't see him well enough to know if it's working. Olivia and Jason turn their lights away from our circle, and I count at least three whitetips circling us. Whitetips can be very curious and aggressive under certain circumstances, but panicking and retreating rapidly typically just draws them closer.

I shine my light down and see a bright red fish laying on its side in the coral. As I pan right, I see one of the bigger moray eels I've ever seen, and it is on the move. It's rare to see a moray out of its hole in the reef, but it seems pretty motivated to beat the sharks to the injured fish, which looks to be a good-sized snapper. I reason that the circling whitetips are likely far more interested in the dying fish than they are in us.

I'm tempted to take control of the group and slowly lead them away from this section of the reef, but I glance back at Jason instead. I notice he is tapping the other divers and motioning to them to follow him. Mark tucks in close behind his son, and Olivia and I fall into line. Once we've moved about twenty yards down the reef, Jason stops and turns to check on us. He signals to check our air pressure by holding his gauge up and gently tapping on the glass face. We've all burned through quite a bit of air in the excitement, especially Mark. Jason motions again for us to follow and leads us slowly back to the anchor line. I'm impressed he found his way back in the dark. He signals up with his thumb, and we all slowly follow him up the anchor line, making a safety stop at fifteen feet before breaking the surface.

"Did you see all of that action?" Jason asks with excitement.

"Amazing!" Olivia says. "Dolphins, mantas, and sharks in the same day...amazing."

"That's very rare," I say.

"I almost lost it there, Morgan," Mark says to me.

"Yes, but you didn't," I respond. "You kept it together and followed our fearless leader over there back to safety." I point toward Jason as we swim toward the stern of the *Hihi'o*.

Back on board, we unload our tanks, dry off, and enter the galley area just as rain begins to fall. Many things could have gone wrong on that dive, but they did not. Jason exhibited some remarkable confidence that somehow translated to the rest of us, especially his father. The risks and the fear were real, but the dive went without any serious problems.

I make a conscious choice to remember this dive. I savor the good dives and learn from the bad ones...in a way, then, all dives are good dives for me. There's a running joke among dive instructors that if your class went smoothly, then beware because the next one will probably be a disaster. There's this belief that somehow the universe balances itself with good and bad experiences, and the more good classes you have, the worse the ones to come will be, like some sort of diving *karma*.

I no longer believe that to be true. Instead, I believe there is a self-fulfilling prophecy whereby the instructor creates bad experiences by believing they are inevitable. This all reminds me of Mark, who seems to manifest bad experiences simply by expecting them to happen. Good and bad can also be a matter of perspective. Spotting a shark on a dive is the worst thing in Mark's world, while it brings Olivia joy.

The trickle of rain turns into a downpour as other divers make their way inside. This is a tropical rain...a hard rain. Mark ducks out of the salon to grab the towel he left on the dive deck. He is smiling when he returns as water drips down his face. A mix of pride and relief seems to be present on his face as he walks to the table where I'm sitting with Olivia and Jason.

"Thanks," is all he says to me, placing his hand on my shoulder. He turns to walk away, and I think I know what he means, but I decide not to press further.

"And thanks for leading us, Jason," Mark says, turning back to face his son.

A look passes between them that is hard to interpret. I can't say I'd seen them even make direct eye contact with each other since boarding the boat. But they are now staring at each other. A smile creeps onto Jason's face. His father responds with an even bigger grin. I'd only seen Mark smile one time before. Olivia is watching the exchange and begins laughing to herself. Something seems to have broken loose between them. I can actually feel a new connection growing between them but can't quite put my finger on it. I self-consciously become aware that I'm shifting my gaze back and forth between the two of them. I start to feel like I'm intruding on an intimate moment between father and son. The voice whispers in my ear, "Transformation takes root when you stop making decisions out of fear and/or denial."

I dismiss my curiosity to ask questions and let us all just feel the moment between them. I stand up to leave but stop moving when

Jason stands up and walks toward his father. I expect them to embrace, but Jason quickly turns his head to say goodnight to me and Olivia then brushes past his father. Mark also says goodnight and follows his son toward the shower area.

"Take a seat, Morgan," Olivia says, patting the chair next to her. A wave of exhaustion sweeps over me, and I don't want to sit back down, but I do. This young woman has some weird power over people.

8

"Why'd you stop going to church?" Olivia asks as I sit down next to her in the salon. I don't immediately respond, so she stands, walks over to pour herself a cup of coffee, then returns to the table and sits down. She peers into my eyes.

"What'd you say?" I finally respond. I'm pretending not to have heard her question, when I'm really just stalling for time to think how far I want to plunge into this topic. Not far, I decide. But I've watched her interact with her father, brother, and other divers, and I gather she's not really the type to stop a line of questioning simply because the other person is not in the mood to talk or is uncomfortable with the subject.

"You heard me," she says with a wry smile on her face. "Answer the question."

The tired soul I keep hidden away since losing my son is draping over my shoulders as I struggle to answer her question. My longing in the moment is to go inside my head where I find solace and rejuvenation. But I'm guessing she'll have none of that. She just stares at me with an expectant look on her face. She's one of those people you can't resist answering. She has an inquisitive mind, a rare ability to be fully present in a moment, and a genuine love for other humans that is tactile. I've observed her talking to other people on the boat...she is very disarming. I suppose that is what makes her a good therapist.

"I'm...I'm not completely sure," I finally say.

"Oh, BS," she says simply, still smiling. "You don't seem like the kind of person who makes rash decisions. You're a thinker...you think about everything you do. I've watched you closely. In fact, you probably *overthink* everything you do."

I start my answer like I start most of my answers...with a story.

"Of all the things Jesus did and said, one of the most fascinating stories to me is the evening He decided to walk on water," I start in.

Olivia's smile grows as I talk. At first, I think it's because she's curious about my story, but I begin to realize she's smiling because she was right when she said I probably overthink everything, this answer being the latest example. I don't care what she's thinking. I continue my story because *I* know *I* need to hear it.

"While most of the miracles attributed to him had a very practical application...healing a sick person, commanding a demon to leave someone alone, feeding thousands of people...this one stands out as kind of peculiar to me. What was the point of walking on water? I know many people just dismiss this story as a fairy tale, but whether you believe it or not, why did his followers decide to include it in the records? Is Jesus just showing off, or maybe making a statement that he and his followers are not even subject to the laws of nature? Is he proving he's really God in the flesh? Is he saying by walking on water that the things we believe are real may, in fact, not be...I've thought a lot about this."

"I can tell," she says sarcastically.

"Even more peculiar to me about this story of Jesus walking on the water," I continue, "is the fact that his disciple Peter decides he wants to walk on the water also. Jesus invites Peter to do so, and Peter takes a few steps before he notices the wind and the waves and begins to sink. So where is Peter's faith as he is sinking? He couldn't have lost faith in Jesus because Jesus isn't sinking. Jesus couldn't have lost faith in Peter because Jesus invited Peter to walk on the water. Peter lost faith in himself that he could do what Jesus had asked him to do. Peter gave in to the fear that what was *outside* of him was greater than what was *inside* of him. At least that's how I've heard it preached."

Olivia sits patiently listening to my round-about answer.

"And why did Peter ask to walk on water in the first place?" I ask rhetorically. "I think he says something like 'If it's you, tell me to come to you on the water.'"

"Not sure where you're going with this, Morgan," she interrupts. "But I mostly think you're dodging the question."

"When my students give in to panic and bolt for the surface, it is because they have lost faith in themselves, not in me," I continue, undeterred. "They've lost faith in their ability to continue doing what is being asked of them, just like your dad did on those first dives. Students come to me because they want to learn to dive. And there's this unspoken agreement between us that if I tell them to do something then they must be able to do it."

"So...you're Jesus in this analogy?" she asks with a note of sarcasm in her voice. But there is a hint of curiosity as well.

"Jesus said, 'Can any one of you by worrying add a single hour to your life?'" I say.

"Umm...now I really don't know what you're talking about, and I still don't think you're answering my question," Olivia cuts in with a more serious look on her face.

I plunge ahead...

"The simple answer to Jesus's question is 'no.' In fact, most of us know the stress that comes with worrying will probably shorten our lives. But *understanding* something intellectually and *feeling* it physically and/or emotionally are often very different things. You are probably going to experience fear and worry in your lifetime, but what you do about it can make all the difference."

"Just *answer* the fucking question," she interrupts. "Why did you stop going to church…why is that so hard for you?"

"I don't completely know," I finally say. "I was raised in a church, went off to college to study theology, figured I would be a pastor at this point in my life." The smile returns to Olivia's face as I sincerely try to answer her question. But the answer that used to seem so clear now evades me. I can see it dimly; I just can't quite grab onto it.

"Do you mean, what were the actual circumstances that led to me leaving the church, or do you just mean philosophically why I don't put myself in that environment anymore?" I ask.

"I can guess the circumstances that led to you leaving. You were probably hurt by someone in the church since you grew up in that environment, most likely some pastor or two somewhere. You probably disappeared from church somewhere in your twenties and then came back when you had kids. Then when your kids grew up, you got into a fight with someone else at church and decided you don't need the grief anymore." Her description is eerily accurate, and I begin to realize my story isn't exactly unique.

"The stories people tell me are either they just never really had any involvement with the church—obviously not you—or some bullshit about how Christians are hypocrites, as if other people outside the church are not. Or someone took advantage of them, which is not bullshit, but is also not limited to people who go to church."

"So, you want my philosophical answer then?" I ask, now laughing. "Fear, I guess."

"Wait…what?" she asks.

"Fear is why I left the church. I never realized it until this moment, but fear is why I left the church. I always end up feeling like the thing God is telling me is way different from the thing the church is telling me. If I do what the church is telling me, it makes people happy and me very unhappy. If I do what God is telling me, it makes me very happy and the church people very unhappy. I just don't like the tension of those two things and go to great lengths to avoid the conflict."

"So, it's the conflict you fear?" she asks.

"I suppose so," I say.

"Do you just not like conflict in general or is there something special about conflict with the church that scares you?"

"All of the above. I don't like conflict in general, but I especially don't like it in the church. It seems like if we're all listening to God, then there should be some agreement. But nothing could be further from the truth," I say. "It's the reason there are so many different kinds of churches. We can't agree on anything. In even more extreme cases, people who think they're listening to God are the ones who start wars. It's like each of us thinks we understand what God is saying better than the other person who thinks they know what God is *really* saying."

"What's it like when God talks to you?" she asks, shifting away from my critique of the modern church.

I am stopped in my tracks. How do I explain the voice? No one ever asks me that specific question.

"It always seems to be about what I'm supposed to do next or who I should encourage or who I can help," I say. "Sometimes it sounds like a riddle for me to solve."

"How does that make you feel?" she asks. "Does that scare you? It would scare me."

"Yes and no," I answer. "I like knowing what God wants me to do, even though I generally don't want to do it. It always seems too big or too impossible or too costly...costly...that's the one that gets me."

"How so?"

"I was hosting this thing with my wife on Thursday nights at my house. We'd invite people over for dinner, then talk about the Bible or pray for people or share or just be there for that one particular person that is stuck."

"Sounds nice," she says.

"It was anything but nice," I answer quickly. "It was nearly impossible. I would lie awake Wednesday nights anticipating Thursday night and what might happen or who might show up. It always seemed so out of control. I'd always have a plan, and that plan always got scrapped by whatever else was going on in people's lives."

"Is it safe to say you *feared* Thursday nights?" she asks. She draws out the word feared, making a point I don't seem to be grasping.

"Feared seems like too strong of a word, but I suppose there was an element of that," I say.

"Sounds like more than an *element* to me if just thinking about it kept you awake the night before. Sounds like maybe fear was the central *element* to what you were feeling. If you feared it so much, why did you do it? Don't think, just answer."

"Same reason I take night dives," I say. Whoops...I may have just admitted to a student that I still experience fear before night dives.

"Wow," she responds. "Your brain is on overdrive with all of this...slow down a sec. You have this way of blurting out all sorts of random statements, then somehow tying it all together if someone is patient enough to listen to the long version of your story. Do you feel misunderstood most of the time?"

"Yes," I answer quickly.

She lets my answer hang in the air without responding. She takes a long sip of her coffee while staring at me. She sets her cup down, glances across the salon, then back at me.

"What do you mean by 'the same reason I take night dives?'"

"I like how I feel afterward," I say.

"See, you're doing it again," she says. "You start at the end of the story, then back up to the beginning. So, you fear the thought of night diving, just like you feared the thought of Thursday nights and of going to church?"

"Again, fear sounds like too strong of a word, but I suppose there's truth in there somewhere," I say.

"Shut up...let me finish," she says as she connects the dots. "You fear the thought of night diving, just like you feared Thursday nights, and you ultimately stopped going to church out of fear, but you did or do them all because you like the way you felt or feel afterward?"

I sit there thinking about the deep truth in what she's saying to me. I stand up and slowly walk across the galley area. I grab a coffee cup and fill it from the metal urn strapped to the bulkhead. I start to walk back to where Olivia is sitting but change my mind and take the coffee back and dump it in the galley sink. I walk over to the refrigerator, grab a beer, and take it back to my seat. She's analyzing every move I make. I start to feel uncomfortable, but I sit back down anyway.

"That was a question, by the way," she says.

I don't answer. I've always thought of fear as the opposite of faith...as in, if I just had enough faith, there would be no fear. As I sit at the table, I realize the opposite of fear is not faith...it's denial.

"I can see a picture in my mind that looks like a timeline," I say. "The word *fear* is on the far-left end of the timeline, and the word *denial* is on the far-right end. Halfway in between is the word *faith*."

Fear .... Faith .... Denial

"Take money, for instance," I continue. "I begin to worry about money and realize I'm giving in to my *fear* that there may not be enough someday. I don't like that feeling and believe it is contrary to *faith*, so I just start pretending that it doesn't bother me and spend recklessly. But that's not *faith*. I've slid from *fear* right past *faith* and into *denial.* On the other hand, if I have stopped moving forward, believing that no matter how I move it will all end in disaster, then I'm giving in to *fear*. *Faith* seems to be in between. It's the ability to thoughtfully consider the challenges in front of me, formulate a plan of attack, then move forward."

"Interesting, but I don't think I really understand what you mean," she says.

"OK, well...another example is night diving," I reply. "Fear looks like sitting in the galley telling others, 'night diving just isn't my thing.' Denial looks like jumping off the boat without a plan or a flashlight, believing my buddy's light will be good enough. Faith is recognizing the risks involved with night diving, ensuring each diver has the proper gear, doing a safety check with my buddy, and planning for contingencies should conditions change during the dive. There's still risk involved, but I'm acknowledging it and mitigating it to the best of my ability. At the same time, I won't let fear keep me out of the water."

"Makes sense," she says. "What was the money part?"

"With money, *fear* looks like hoarding my resources, worrying there might not be enough; *denial* looks like recklessly spending my resources or worse, borrowing on credit, saying things like, 'God will provide,' or believing that I'll always be in debt, so who cares if it's five thousand dollars or five hundred thousand dollars. Faith lies in the middle...having an actual plan for the resources and training made available to me in the moment, and then moving forward with flexibility in the plan, trusting that the part I cannot yet see will reveal itself along the way."

"Wow, again, you've thought about this a lot," Olivia says.

"Actually, no. This is all occurring to me as I tell it to you," I say.

"I call bullshit," she says, shooting me a quizzical look. "You expect me to believe you just *now* thought of all of this?"

"OK, I've probably thought about all this before, but I've never really said it. Hearing it out loud as I tell you...I don't know...it's just hitting me differently. That's why it sounds so scattered. I always hear the conclusion first, then the story writes itself in my brain to explain the ending."

"So that's the voice of God you were talking about?" she asks.

"Yes!" I respond. "At least that's what it seems like to me. I know it sounds weird, so I don't talk about it much. But hey...you asked."

A weary look passes over her face, and I immediately think I've said too much.

"It's surprising how tired diving makes me," Olivia says, changing the subject.

"Everybody says that," I say. "Some of it has to do with the internal workout for your lungs and heart that comes with breathing dense air at depth. But most of the fatigue comes from teaching your body to do something that is not in its nature...breathing underwater. It takes a mental and physical toll."

"Could be," she says. "Either way, I'm going to bed." She stands up, puts her hand on my shoulder, says goodnight, and walks off to the bunk area.

I return her goodnight, finish my beer, and head to my bunk as well.

I lay down in my bunk, and my brain starts to ramp up. *Not now...I want to sleep*, I say to myself as the wheels start to churn in my head. Do I really believe what I just said about faith? Does is apply to the non-diving side of my life also? I spend most of my time running the businesses that I've started. That technically makes me an entrepreneur, but I don't tend to think of myself that way. The business ideas always seem to pop into my head out of nowhere (the voice?), and I pursue them reluctantly. Instead of excitement, I more often feel a sense of responsibility to pursue these ideas. Mary is very supportive and helps tremendously, but she tells me she feels more like she's just being dragged along on these adventures. I don't think she's a willing participant, but I don't really think I am either. The *fear, faith, denial* timeline reappears in my mind, and it occurs to me that the goal is not to move from one end to the other, as with most timelines, but to remain in the center. I drift off to sleep to the sound of the heavy rain that is still falling on the deck and the rocking of the boat as wind continues to drive the storm onto the coast.

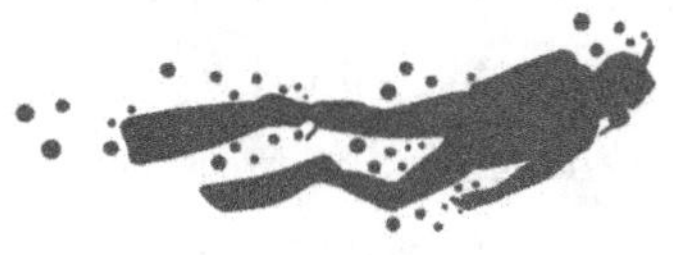

9

The predawn light spills into the bunk room as I wake up on day five. The storm from last night has blown by, and I can tell the sky is blue without even looking outside. It's a blue-sky day...I can feel it somewhere inside of me. Immediately, my brain starts to churn. A few pressing needs of my current small businesses come to mind, but I push them to the side to refocus on what I believe will be a good day of diving.

What is it about diving that has kept it so central to me for decades? And why teach others to dive? I had been diving most of my life and earned a college degree and remember thinking it couldn't be that hard to take the classes and pass the exam to become a PADI instructor...right? The short answer? Harder than I thought, but not for the reason I thought.

As I began to look into the process so many years ago, I found out there were numerous steps I needed to take along the way. I also quickly realized that pursuing the goal bit-by-bit on my free weekends was going to take me nearly a year to complete. First, although I had been diving for years, I had to go back and get an advanced diver certification, then a rescue diver certification, then become a divemaster for a while, including several internships and evaluations by instructors. Then I needed to take a five-day, eight-hours-a-day course, followed by a two-day examination in a classroom, pool, and the ocean. Not that onerous in comparison to other training regimes I've seen, but why add the unneeded stress to my already busy life of working full-time and raising my young family?

Aside from the schedule, two other things really threw me during this process. The first was the realization that I could not pass the instructor course without some pretty serious studying of diving and decompression theory (I hadn't studied like that since college). The second realization, which was far more profound for me, was that I would have to become much more aware of other divers around me.

I had been diving so long that it was second nature to me. I could dive without much conscious thought of my technique, breathing, buoyancy, and other factors that affect divers. But as I took more classes on my way to becoming an instructor, I began to realize that while I could help myself in an emergency, I wouldn't be of much help to anyone else if they had a problem. Self-preservation came naturally to me, but I needed to be intentionally trained to put others' needs before my own.

The first and possibly only time I had considered another life more important than my own was the day my son James was born. More significantly, I remember the day *after* he was born. That was the day I learned about the "anomalies" in his body. After Mary shared the news of what the doctor said, I raced to the natal unit to get a better look at him. I noticed his arms and legs were somewhat different from the other babies, and a cloud of confusion descended on me.

I walked out of the natal unit and started down a hallway, not sure of where I was heading. As I walked in a daze, the hallway floor seemed to be rising. It wasn't until I finally reached the end of the hallway that I understood that the floor was not actually rising. I was falling to my knees and crawling to the end of the hallway, where I collapsed, sobbing onto the stained industrial carpet.

"Please, God, no," was all I could utter. "Anything, God. Take anything from me to make him whole. If it's my fault, then take my life and make him well." I had never had a thought like that in my life. I loved Mary and I loved her two young children from a previous marriage, who I now considered my own. But before the moment of gazing upon my biological son and seeing the physical challenges I imagined would be part of his ongoing life, I can't say I'd ever had the conscious thought of being willing to sacrifice my life for another.

Mary was my opposite. I could never get her to put herself first. She naturally sacrificed everything for her children and even strangers from time to time. She had often told me I became a much better dive buddy to her only after I was trained to pay attention to other divers. But I'm still not sure that training translated into me being a better partner to her in life.

"Why do you look at the speck of sawdust in your brother's eye and pay no attention to the plank in your own eye?" Jesus's words float through my head. "... you hypocrite, first take the plank out of your own eye, and then you will see clearly to remove the speck from your brother's eye."

I had heard these words as a child and have always thought this was a warning not to judge other people. While it is true that I should not judge others, there is a more subtle secondary instruction: Once I've dealt with my own issues, I also actually need to be available to help others deal with their issues. I typically got so wrapped up in dealing with my own stuff that I never got around to helping anyone else. Learning to teach others would have to be a breakthrough for me.

To become a scuba instructor, I needed to first work out all of my hidden shortcomings through strenuous physical and mental testing. I can remember being in water so cold I could no longer feel my hands while hauling a diver, who was pretending to be unconscious, several hundred yards back to the beach, all the while striping off his gear and providing rescue breaths. There were times I wasn't sure I could finish. I took two days of exams, both written and physical, knowing that if I failed even one part, I would fail the entire testing and have to start all over again.

Once I made it through, I felt competent to not only deal with my own problems but, more important, with other people's problems in the water. The process also taught me how to be patient with others who just couldn't seem to get the hang of diving. It taught me when to push people to reach beyond what they thought they were capable of doing and also when to provide comfort and patience in their failure, preparing them to *fight* another day.

But the real-life lesson I learned in all of that was I had a "plank" stuck in my own eye that was preventing me from seeing the "specks" in others' eyes. The plank was complete self-absorption to the point of not even being aware there were others around me. Even after all the training, in the first few years of teaching, I was still more conscious of *impressing* students with my flawless technique than how and what my students were actually learning. I didn't see my own ego until some patient instructors came alongside me and taught me to be even more aware of others around me.

The life I had always wanted was in service to others. But to get there, I had to transfer the knowledge of my own diving techniques to my students, remembering to make the experience about them and not about me. That was a life worth living.

The familiar smell of bacon frying wafts into my bunk, signaling the start of another day of diving. It is time to get out of bed and out of my brain. I get up, stop by the head, then make my way to the galley area. Only Jason is at the table. Mark and Olivia don't appear to be up yet.

"Morning," I say to Jason.

"Good morning," he replies, more warmly than usual. "How was your night?"

"Not bad...although I did more thinking than sleeping. I always seem to do a lot of thinking on dive boats."

"This is the first time I've been on a dive boat," Jason says, "but I've been doing a lot of thinking too."

He wants to talk, which seems odd. He hasn't said much to me on this trip—or to anyone else for that matter—but it feels like he has a question.

"Lemme grab a cup of coffee," I say, walking across the galley. He waits patiently for me. He's watching my every move. I get my coffee and return to the table.

"Can I ask you something?" Jason says. "Let me know if I'm asking too much or if you don't feel like talking about it."

"Um...OK," I say. I'm definitely paying attention now, curious as to what he's going to ask.

"I'm kind of wondering how you dealt with losing your son," he says.

"Oh, you want to have *that* talk," I say, more to myself than to Jason. "Well first...what do you mean by 'dealt with losing your son?'"

"Like I said, if this is too much, you can tell me," he replies. "But my friend died in a car wreck about three years ago, and it kinda messed me up. I miss him a lot, and the pain seems to be getting worse, not better. I'm just curious how you deal with the pain of losing your son."

I'm reminded that learning to dive, especially when you're trapped on a boat for a few days, brings out unexpected conversations at the oddest times. I expect it, yet it somehow always surprises me.

"When my son died, it felt like my life slammed into a wall," I say. "Everything stopped. More accurately, I stopped while everything around me kept flying by. I told my wife once that if I had had a regular job then, instead of being self-employed, I would have been fired for sure. I couldn't function at all. I mean…I could go through the motions of life, get up in the morning, drink coffee, pretend to work, pretend to have meaningful conversations with people throughout the day. But not much had any purpose to me anymore. I kept asking myself, 'What is the point to all of this…what is the point of my life anymore?' I wouldn't say I was suicidal, but I remember thinking that if I just didn't happen to wake up the next day, I'd be OK with it. I know we all die, but it should be in order. When I lost my father, I was sad, but it made sense to me. He was in his 90s, he'd had a long, fruitful life. There's supposed to be some sort of age order to dying. But my son…he was only twenty-three. He had just graduated from college two weeks before he died. He had earned his degree and was starting his life. He had asked me about helping him start a business, and I was excited to work with him. Then it all just got…got…taken away. I'm not really sure how I got through the pain or continue to get through the pain. I just get up every day and decide to live."

"What happened to him?" Jason asks. "I mean, if you don't mind telling me."

"We're pretty open about it," I say. "He was out fishing with his older brother near Catalina Island off the coast of Los Angeles in a boat that was too small for what they were doing. They both went overboard in a fluke accident. His older brother Ben tried to save him, but it wasn't to be…we never saw him again. He just vanished off the face of the earth. Fortunately, his brother somehow made it back onto the boat or we would have lost him too, and maybe we would have never found out what happened."

"Wow…I had no idea," Jason responds. Tears begin to well up in his eyes. I know I'm telling a sad story, but there seems to be years of pain behind his tears. The pain of losing his friend, the pain of his parent's divorce…maybe other pain I didn't know about.

"Tell me about your friend," I say, shifting the conversation back to Jason.

"I'd known him nearly all my life," he says. "We met in first grade and stayed friends our whole lives." He stops talking as if deciding whether or not he wants to continue his story.

"What happened to him?" I ask, gently encouraging him to go on.

"We were at a party that night," he continues. "We were all drinking and definitely drunk. My memories of that night are all hazy, but I had promised his mom to look out for Matty that night. His name was Matthew, but I always called him Matty. At some point, I passed out on a couch, but Matty kept on drinking. My friends said Matty decided to go home, and he got in my car...we had taken my car that night...a seventy Chevelle I rebuilt with my dad. He got behind the wheel, but he didn't get far without my car keys. They said I somehow woke up, went outside, and tried to get him out of the driver's seat. Matty got out and snatched the keys from me, my friends said, and told me I was too drunk to drive. I guess I wrestled with him over the keys before he got them away from me. Then he pushed me over into a flower bed next to the driveway."

He's having trouble telling his story and begins to choke up. He stops talking and looks at me like he's searching for something...maybe an answer to his painful question? An answer I must somehow have after surviving the death of my son.

"Then what happened?" I ask.

"I don't really remember, but my friends said they tried to get the keys from Matty...but they were pretty drunk too. He got away from them and drove off in my car. No one knew it at the time, but I got up out of the flower bed and got into the back seat...no small trick in a two-door car."

Tears well up in his eyes, and he has to stop to catch his breath.

"He got on the freeway in the wrong direction and drove straight into an oncoming car...a minivan with a mom, dad, and three kids. Everybody died, including Matty and the whole family. Well...not everybody died. I survived, but I was pretty messed up and spent weeks in the hospital. I should have died."

Jason looks across the galley, then back at me. We sit there for a minute, staring at each other. I don't have an answer for him. I don't even know how to respond. But I imagine he's wondering why he survived and not his friend.

"His family thought of me as another son," he says. "I went on their family vacations...I even dated his sister for a while, and I think they thought I was going to marry into their family. Now they don't even talk to me. They knew Matty had a drinking problem, and I was usually the one who kept it together and got him home safely. I promised his mom I would do the same as usual that night, but I didn't."

"So, you think it was your fault?" I ask.

"I *know* it was my fault!" he says a bit too loudly. "Everyone tells me it wasn't my fault, but I know it was."

He gets up from the table and walks over to get himself more coffee. His pain reminds me of my older son Ben's pain at losing his brother. He blames himself also. Mary and I have never thought he was responsible for his brother's death, but it doesn't change the way he feels. I'm curious if Matty's family no longer speaks to Jason because they think he was responsible for Matty's death or because he is such a strong reminder of who they lost. Pain over losing a child is very disorienting. It breaks people. It destroys relationships. It devastates marriages. It changes people so profoundly that some simply can't go on.

Jason looks back at me sitting at the table. He takes a couple steps in my direction, then turns, and heads out onto the dive deck. He's talking to himself, a curious look on his face, as if he might be wondering why he told me all this. I have a feeling he doesn't talk about this with anyone and is regretting telling me. I sip my now-cold coffee.

"Good morning," Mark says as he sits across the table from me. He takes off his sunglasses and looks at me, waiting for a response.

"Oh...uh...good morning," I say back to him.

"What's up with Jason?" Mark asks. "I passed him on the dive deck and said good morning. He acted like he didn't even see me."

"I'm not sure. But he was telling me about his accident," I say.

"Oh...with Matty?" Mark says. "Yeah, that's been pretty tough on him. He's never been the same ever since. He used to be pretty outgoing before that...you know, the life of the party...chatting everyone up...the first to start a conversation with anybody. He's pretty quiet now, as you can tell. Last night's dive was the first time I've seen him take some initiative in a long time."

"Yes," is all I say.

"It's been pretty hard on all of us, to tell you the truth," Mark continues. "Matty's family thought of Jason as one of their own, but we thought the same way about Matty. Those two were inseparable. Our two families didn't have much in common, so we didn't hang out much...but those two were definitely brothers."

"Why were your families so different?" I ask.

"You know...we were church people and all that...and they...well they were the *sinners* we weren't supposed to be hanging out with."

"The *sinners*?" I ask.

"Yeah, you know...never went to church...had a bunch of failed marriages between the two parents...drank too much...their kids partied...they cursed a lot...*sinners*. It seems pretty ridiculous now, considering I don't go to church anymore, I'm divorced, and I probably drink too much."

"And your daughter swears a lot," I say, smiling.

"Holy shit. Are you fuckers talking about me behind my back?" Olivia shouts from the other side of the galley area. She's getting coffee and smiling to herself. She has very good hearing and an even better sense of timing.

"True," Mark says. "Funny part is she's the only one who still goes to church."

"What's on the dive slate for today?" Mark asks, making a U-turn in the conversation.

"We're going to work on navigation," I respond. "I'll explain more when everyone's here, but I'm going to teach you how to navigate underwater so you don't get lost when you start diving without me."

He nods, apparently satisfied with my short answer. He gets up and walks over to where Olivia is standing by the coffee pot. They're talking about something. It seems serious, and they speak quietly. I wonder if he's telling her about my conversation with Jason. Mark looks back at me, hesitates, then turns, and walks back to the stairs leading down to the bunk room. Olivia looks at me, smiles, and walks over to sit down.

"Good morning, divemaster," she says enthusiastically.

"It's instructor," I say.

"What did you say?" she asks.

"I said, it's instructor, not divemaster. Divemaster would be a demotion," I say with mock indignation.

"Divemaster sounds more important...kinda like master of the universe or something," she says.

"It's not...divemasters assist instructors, not the other way around. We say divemaster is the *first* level in professional diving."

She's staring at me with a curious look, like she's trying to figure out if I'm actually offended.

"I'm not that easily offended," I say to break the silent stare. "What I said is true, but I'm just messing with you…lots of people get that mixed up."

"Oh, OK," she says. "You can be a little hard to read sometimes. The expression on your face doesn't always seem to match how you say you're feeling."

She's not the first person to tell me that about myself. I've often wondered if the expression on my face matches what I've been thinking about in the past or what is to come versus what I'm experiencing in the moment. I'm not sure what that says about me, but it must be true for so many people to comment on it. Olivia's face, on the other hand, is an open book. Her expression always seems to exactly match whatever is happening in the moment. That might be why people like to talk to her…she's very present in the moment.

"So…Jason told you his story?" she asks.

"Yes, he did," I answer. "At least most of it. The stress of learning how to dive seems to have that effect on people. It's like some sort of weird truth serum."

"Our family has all sorts of little secrets," she says as she sips her coffee. "Did he tell you mine?"

"You have a secret?" I ask.

"Well…for most of my life I did. I don't anymore." She continues to sip her coffee and shifts her chair so she can see out onto the dive deck.

"Are you going to tell me?" She definitely has my attention now. There's something about secrets that get people's attention.

"My wife says I have lots of secrets," she says.

"Really? You don't seem like the kind of person who has lots of secrets," I say. "Oh…you just said your wife…so your secret is the fact that you're attracted to women...that's your big secret?"

"It definitely was in our family," she answers. "Remember, we were the nice little Christian family...the ones who always went to church...tithed...didn't drink...didn't swear...didn't sleep around. I knew pretty early on that I liked girls, but that wasn't really presented to me as a life option the way I grew up."

"That must have been complicated," I reply.

I can't actually imagine how difficult that had been for her to grow up in an atmosphere that condemned the very person she believed herself to be. It's interesting that she's the only one in her family who is still a part of a church. I can't understand what she went through any more than she can understand how it was for me to lose a child or for Jason to go through his ordeal or for Mark to lose his marriage. Pain is not something easily measured or compared. I can't measure my pain against Olivia's because there is no standard of pain; there's no objective scale by which it can be measured. Pain is an intensely personal experience. I don't even know which is worse, physical or psychological pain. So...is the instruction to not judge others simply a realization of the fact that none of us completely understands what other people are going through?

"Is it still difficult?" I ask.

"Depends on who I'm around," she answers. Now, for the second time since I met her, Olivia's smile is gone. "I mean, I know I still have friends who think what I'm doing is wrong...or 'sinful.' I don't know...let's talk about diving."

"Sure," I say. "Let's talk about diving. Diving is the great equalizer. When we dive, we are all literally in over our heads, putting ourselves in the same circumstance. And we all want the same thing...air. Breathing is everything. Some people get a little uppity about who is smoothest at buoyancy control or who is the best at conserving air, but the ones who brag the most are typically the ones who get into trouble first.

"The best divers don't talk about their capabilities much and are the most ready to help others on their way to becoming better divers. Underwater, it doesn't matter much what sex you are, who you're attracted to, if you're old or young, have a dark past, or what race you happen to be...you're either breathing underwater or you're not. And if you stop breathing, the job of everyone around you is to get you breathing again."

"That's a lot of stuff you just said there," Olivia says.

I glance away from her as Mark and Jason return from the dive deck and sit down at our table. I look beyond our group and see that most of the people in the galley area are listening in on our conversation. Maybe that's why Olivia changed the subject?

I've been passionate about diving my entire life, and it comes out of me like a river at times. I use that passion to explain everything in my life. It's so important to me, and I now know why...diving is the way I look at the world and everyone around me. And teaching others to dive makes me a better version of myself. Diving continues to teach me that we're all somehow in the same water in life and on the same journey, even though each of our circumstances look very different. The only real job we have is to help each other breathe.

"So, let's talk about navigation," I say, looking around the table. "First of all, don't be afraid of small mistakes."

"Aren't we trying to avoid mistakes?" Mark asks.

"Big ones, yes," I answer. "But little ones may just be course corrections...like steering a car."

"I thought you said diving is like driving a boat, not a car," Jason says.

"I said *buoyancy control* is like driving a boat to try to explain anticipating changes by working on breath control and not overcorrecting," I reply. "But navigation is more like steering a car down the freeway, correcting thousands of mistakes each minute. You're really not *doing something* as much as you are *preventing something.* Assuming you don't have a self-driving car, take your hands off the wheel and watch what happens. Your car continuously wants to go the wrong direction, so you make thousands of small corrections based on the constant feedback you are receiving from the road, the wheel, and your gauges. Make enough corrections to keep it on the road and you will reach your final destination. Just like learning to drive, go slow and make small corrections while you're learning to navigate and you'll get there."

"Makes sense," Mark says. "So, what are we actually going to do?"

"I'm going to teach you how to navigate back and forth in a straight line using a compass to refresh some of what you learned in the open water course," I say. "Then I'll show you how to measure distance by counting the number of kick cycles it takes to cover a hundred feet underwater."

"What's a kick cycle?" Jason asks.

"You count a kick cycle every time one of your feet returns to its starting point," I say. "So, if you start with your right foot below your left, you'd count a cycle each time your right foot returns to that position." They all appear satisfied with my explanation, so I continue. "Ultimately, you will learn how to navigate in a square pattern by making three ninety-degree turns in sequence to return to your starting point. I'll also show you some things about natural navigation using currents, landmarks, depths, and patterns in the sand."

These navigation dives often become competitive. The divers like to compare results to see who was able to navigate and end up closest to the designated ending point. Divers also tend to swim far too fast when learning to navigate and become so fixated on their compass that they forget about their buddies, losing them somewhere along the route.

The aim of these navigation dives, in most divers' minds, is to learn how to know where you are underwater and return safely to your exit. Those things are true, but there is a secondary lesson to be learned that is just as important: Learn to lead effectively. I have them take turns leading the dive not only to teach them how to navigate but also to teach them how to effectively care for their buddies. The diver who is best with the compass is not the best leader if they lose their buddy in the process of navigating the dive.

"I'm gonna go downstairs and change into my swimsuit," I say, wrapping up my briefing. "Let's meet on the dive deck in ten minutes."

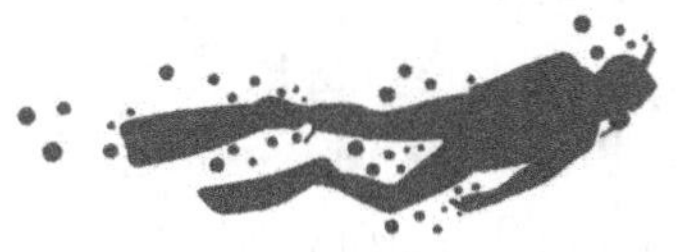

10

Sunlight is flooding the dive deck as we emerge from the salon. A gentle breeze from the south fails to push the growing heat on the deck over the side of the boat. We quickly suit up and jump into the water. I lead them over to a shallow area nearer to the shore that is mostly sandy. There are fewer obstacles to bump into and no fragile life on the bottom to destroy if they lose control of their buoyancy while concentrating on navigation. I anchor a thin line on the bottom and have them swim along it counting kick cycles.

After counting kick cycles down the line and back to the starting place, we return to the surface. I give them some instruction on their compasses about making three ninety-degree turns to navigate in a square pattern. I then turn them loose, with Mark leading the first go-round, while I wait for them at the surface near a small marker buoy attached by an additional line to their starting point on the bottom.

"Great job on navigating the course," I say to Mark as he surfaces several minutes later about a yard away from me. "But where are Olivia and Jason?"

"Uh...well...they were right behind me," he responds. "At least I thought they were behind me."

"This is a buddy sport, remember," I say. "If you lose your buddies while leading the dive, then you failed."

"Yeah…where are they?" He asks, scanning the horizon.

"How would you find them if I wasn't here?" I ask.

"I'm…I'm not sure how to find them," he says, slowly turning in a circle. "Should I go looking for them on the bottom?"

"Just sit still here in the water with me," I reply. "Hopefully, they remember the rule that if they haven't seen you in more than a minute, then they should surface so you can reunite." It's a beautiful day with only a few small swells gently lifting us up and down. "You can also look for disturbances in the water."

"You mean like bubbles?"

"If you're looking down from a boat, you can see divers' bubbles rising to the surface. But from the water it can be much harder to detect bubbles. They can almost look like something swimming just under the surface."

"Like that?" he asks, pointing to a spot about ten feet behind me.

Olivia and Jason slowly break the surface and inflate their BCs.

"What happened?" Olivia asks after gently removing the regulator from her mouth.

"You guys didn't keep up," Mark answers.

I'm reminded of the first dives I ever made with Mary off a small boat on Maui. She told me at the end of the dive that I kept swimming off without her. She couldn't swim as fast as I could underwater, and I would forget to wait for her. If she had a problem underwater, I would never be there to help her. I had to be *taught* to be attentive… so I try to be patient with Mark.

"Wait a sec," I say to him. "You think it's their fault that you all got separated on that dive?"

"Well…yeah, sorta," he responds. "They were supposed to follow me."

Jason and Olivia look at me and roll their eyes, as if in some way, this is the story of their lives. I let the moment pass and instruct Mark to again navigate the course I've laid out for them. I tell him this time to keep track of the buddies he is leading. He does better on the second and third tries, but Olivia and Jason still have trouble keeping up. When they take turns leading the navigation dive, Olivia and Jason's compass skills are clearly not as accurate as their father's, and they have to surface a few times to regain their bearings and get back on course. But I also notice that each time they surface, their buddies are right there with them and not left behind in a cloud of billowing sand.

They all eventually complete the necessary steps of the navigation dive, and they are beginning to run low on air, so we begin a slow swim back to the boat.

"So, which is worse, bad navigation or leaving your buddies behind?" Mark asks as we swim.

"Neither of those things are good, but losing your buddy is worse," I say. "If you stay with your buddy, at least the two of you are *together* to figure out where you are."

We swim in silence back to the *Hibi'o,* where we climb the ladders and make our way back onto the dive deck. We all wriggle out of our gear and strip down our wetsuits.

"Join me on the sundeck and we'll do a little debrief of that dive," I say. I head off and stick my head in the outdoor shower before I start climbing the ladder to the upper deck. Mark, Olivia, and Jason follow. We find partially-shaded seats near the wheelhouse.

"Before you get started, Morgan," Mark says. "I want to say something. I saw the little look my kids gave you after I left them in the dust on that first navigation dive, like they were somehow trying to tell you that I've done this to them before. I'm not an idiot...I am aware of what's going on around me, contrary to what you all think."

"What we all think?" I ask quizzically.

"Their mom used to always say that I only seemed to be aware of myself, and if I was ever aware of other people, it was just to point out their shortcomings."

"Is that true?" I ask. "I mean...you did blame Jason and Olivia for not keeping up with you on the navigation dive."

"*No*, that's not true!" he says, standing to his feet. The tone and volume in his voice are rising.

"Sorry. I'm not accusing you of something," I say to de-escalate the conversation. "I'm legitimately asking a question...do you think your family believes that you mostly care about yourself?"

"I suppose so," he says, collapsing back into his seat.

"Did you say, 'yes?'" I ask. "Sorry, I'm having trouble hearing you all of a sudden."

A look of discovery mixed with confusion washes over his face. Olivia and Jason fix their gaze on their father.

"You really think that's how my family sees me?" he asks, looking back at me.

"Well, what I've learned about the three of you over the past several days gives me the impression that's what they think. They're sitting right there. Ask them."

"I think that's pretty sad if they actually think that about me," he says, turning his head toward his children. "I mean...what does that make me, some kind of dictator?"

We sit in silence for a minute or two while he contemplates this revelation.

"I wonder if that's what my ex—I mean, their mom—meant when she'd say, 'It's always about the money with you?'" he asks himself.

"What about the money?" I ask. Olivia and Jason remain silent.

"Oh, she would always say I cared more about money than my own family. She never understood that the reason I cared about money was *for* my family. I wanted them to have things I never had growing up. I grew up in a military family. My dad joined the Navy at eighteen and met my mom at a bar in San Diego somewhere. He stayed in the Navy as a petty officer, so his salary was always pretty meager. They married young and had five kids, and it seemed like there was never enough to go around—you know, powered milk, canned food—that sort of stuff. I mean, they loved us and all, but there was never any extra money. I wanted something better for my family."

"And was it?" I ask.

"And was it what?" he responds.

"Was it better for your family?"

"Absolutely...it was *waaay* better for them. They had all kinds of things I never had."

"Did they have *you*?" I ask.

"No," Jason interrupts, clearly agitated. "You were never there; you were always at work or something."

"That's not true," Mark responds. "I was always there for you."

"Not really," Jason says. "You were mostly off working to make another buck. You gave us a good life financially, and it might have worked if you *actually* came home once in a while. But even when you were home it seemed like you were mostly thinking about work."

"I wanted to make sure you had more than I had," Mark says.

"We had more than enough," Olivia says, turning to look at Mark. "We *always* had more than enough, but we never had you."

A flash of anger passes over Mark's face, then softens as he starts to tear up. This revelation seems to be more than he can handle.

"So, you're saying I left you behind?" Mark asks his children weakly.

"Not completely," Jason responds. "It was kind of like that dive with the compasses. You were always so fixated on where we were going that you never stopped to see if any of us were actually following you. Olivia and I mostly kept up because we wanted your approval so badly, but mom completely gave up somewhere along the way."

The emotion rolls over Mark as his life replays before his eyes. A tear rolls down his cheek. In the short time we've been together, I have gotten the impression he's not too concerned about what people think of him, which doesn't exactly endear him to me. I sort of figured he would ditch his kids on the navigation dive, but I'm surprised again by his tears and apparent remorse. Even if he doesn't care what others think, he does seem to care what his children think.

"When you finally came around, you always had this way of talking to us—well, more like talking *at* us—that left us feeling judged by you instead of accepted by you," Olivia says.

"What are you talking about?" Mark interjects. The agitated look returns to his face. "When you came out as gay, that was a pretty big deal. I think I handled that pretty well and tried hard not to judge you."

"Do you hear what you're saying?" Olivia says. The therapist is in session. "You *tried* not to judge me. You never really said anything negative to me, but the look you gave me was one of disbelief...kinda like you felt like you never knew me. I'll never forget it. I was still the same person. There was just a part of my life that you never seemed to see."

"What was I supposed to do?" Mark asks. "Your mom was totally freaked out."

"Don't drag her into this," Jason interjects defensively. "You always blame her for everything."

"Look, I'm not blaming your mom," Mark says. "We were already having issues and didn't really know how to talk to each other about any of this stuff."

"I know," Olivia replies. "I overheard the two of you several times asking each other what happened. You didn't say it, but I knew you were wondering at that moment where you went wrong as parents. I knew you were questioning yourself, but it felt like judgment against me."

"You thought the same thing about me when I started hanging out with Matty's family," Jason adds. "Back when we were a nice, little Christian family, Matty's family were clearly the kind of people we weren't supposed to be hanging out with. I knew how you and mom felt about them...like they somehow weren't good enough for us."

"Now who's judging who?" Mark asks Olivia and Jason. "You're judging me. I was just trying to provide a living for my family and working my ass off to make sure you had things I never did. Sorry if I didn't show all the *right* emotions at exactly the *right* time."

Olivia drops her head and raises her hands in a sign of surrender. Jason is staring over the side of the boat toward the coastline. Olivia drops her hands and slowly raises her head. She looks back at her father, searching for something in his eyes.

"I love you, Dad," Olivia says. Her eyes begin to moisten. "We're not judging you. We're telling you we need you. We want you. We love you."

Silence falls over our little group. I suddenly feel like I really shouldn't be in this circle. This is not a dive debriefing, it's a family meeting. I feel like an outsider who is eavesdropping. I shift in my seat, getting ready to stand, and leave them to some privacy.

"I'm glad you're sitting here with us," Olivia says, grabbing my hand. "We needed someone willing to sit through this with us. We know you don't have any answers for us, but you shared your pain and were willing to be part of an event that would make us face these things in our family head-on."

"I agree," says Jason. "I appreciate what you've done for us."

"I…I haven't done anything for you," I stammer.

"Even if you don't feel like you've done much," Jason says, "you made yourself available to us and at least got us talking."

Mark says nothing and looks at me inquisitively as if he can't decide if it's a good or bad thing that I've somehow entered their family dynamic.

"I was never looking for you to solve all my problems or provide everything I ever wanted, Dad," Oliva says. She's looking at Mark but still holding my hand. "I always just wanted you. My favorite memories were the times I saw you laugh and just enjoy life with us. Your joy brings me joy. That was the hardest part of your divorce from mom… just seeing the both of you so sad and broken made it hard for me to find joy in my life. I was so glad when you suggested this dive trip. I really thought I would see the joy return to your eyes, but I've mostly seen self-doubt and fear. Maybe it's too much to ask."

Her statement hangs in the air as a cloud over the sundeck. I'm aware that others are listening, riveted by the breakthrough this family is experiencing. I turn my head and notice some sitting nearby are actually forming tears, overwhelmed by the truth that is being exposed.

"Transformation changes the way you see other people," the voice whispers in my ear.

Then, like turning the lights on in a dark room, the conversation abruptly ends. Olivia lets go of my hand, and we each make our way down the ladder from the sundeck. I head to the bow alone and lose track of the others. It feels like surgery has been performed and only time will reveal whether or not it was a successful procedure.

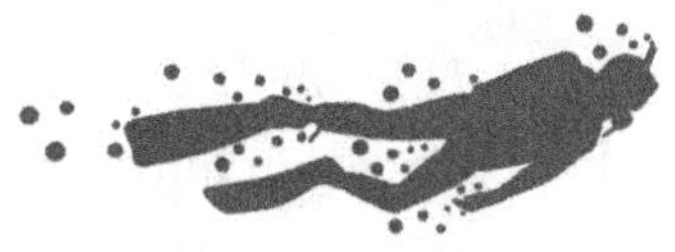

11

"So, what's the secret to life, Morgan?" Olivia asks, joining me on the limited bench seating near the bow of the dive boat. She has a beer in her right hand and offers me the one in her other hand. She's sitting so close that her leg is touching mine. *Odd*, I'm thinking, but she doesn't even seem to notice.

As the sun settles onto the water, I take a long pull on the ice-cold beer and take a deep breath. I realize I've been sitting on the bow for hours as the voice whispers in the breeze, "When grace rules your life, you come into a place of abundance." Profound, I suppose, but very confusing for me. What is it about a sunset that makes most people stop, take a deep breath, and stand still for a moment to witness the sun sinking below the horizon? So much hope for a new day tomorrow.

"The secret to *my* life or the secret to *any* life?" I finally say, never taking my eyes off the sunset. The water shimmers in the fading sun rays as a gentle breeze pushes a washboard ripple across the surface.

"Hmm...let's start with your life," she answers, shifting her gaze from me to what is shaping up to be a dazzling sunset with streaks of purple, red, and yellow stretching across the horizon.

"I don't know if it's the secret," I say, "but the driving force in my life is definitely curiosity."

"Curiosity about what?" she asks.

"Everything," I respond. "My whole life...the thing that drives me forward has always been curiosity. If I'm curious, there's no stopping me. I'm the one who keeps asking questions until I understand. It's what made me a good newspaper reporter."

"You were a newspaper reporter?" she asks. She looks at me and nods her head, as if that somehow better explains me to her.

"Yes...and also an editor for about ten years before taking a job in the heart of Silicon Valley."

"Why'd you stop being a reporter?" she asks.

"You mean other than the fact that newspapers have gone the way of the dinosaurs?" I ask rhetorically. "I was always very good at capturing other people's stories in print. I could ask all kinds of questions about them and keep asking until I cut through the facade most people put up and get to the person underneath."

"That's what made you a good reporter," she says. "But I asked why you stopped."

"So, I'm interviewing this relatively successful, young entrepreneur one day," I answer. "He'd invented some telephone device long before wireless phones were everywhere. And I'm thinking, 'This guy's really not that smart, but he seems to be succeeding, and he's happy with what he's doing and this life he's created.' I realized that day I was spending more time *observing* other people's lives rather than *living* my own. I wanted to *do* something, not just watch others *do* something."

"So, what did you do?" Olivia asks. She looks down at her leg, which is still touching mine, and scoots back a bit on the bench.

"After spending all that time writing for newspapers, I was offered an opportunity to start putting print newspapers online in the early 1990s, so I jumped. I had played around before with the internet, which was mostly just very basic websites with small audiences at that time, but I knew it would be the future. I could clearly see that information flow would no longer just be certain institutions broadcasting information to the masses. I saw that the masses themselves would be trading and transacting information directly...for good or for bad. So, I learned some computer coding and took over the online department of the newspaper I was working for at the time. But I still knew there was more outside the confines of the corporate newspaper environment. I wanted to pursue ideas of my own, which couldn't happen while I was sitting in endless meetings at some giant company. My curiosity about this new medium eventually drove me into a startup tech company in the Silicon Valley of the San Francisco Bay Area. I've made my living from the internet ever since.

"What about diving?" she asks.

"What *about* diving?" I repeat back to her.

"It just seems important to you. Why didn't you make that your career?"

"Same reason I never became a paid minister, even after getting a degree in theology...it was too important to me to make a living at it. There's something about doing an activity primarily for money that ruins it for me. Money always spoils the spiritual nature of things for me. I started teaching scuba around that same time, and I still make a little money at it, but I never wanted to depend on it to make a living. At the same time, it takes me all over the world and I get to meet fascinating people like you."

She rolls her eyes at my last comment. I'm waiting for a deluge of questions, but she seems satisfied with my answer. She stares straight off the bow at the lights from a sailboat slowly motoring by.

"What about you?" I ask. "Why psychology?"

"Curiosity is a big driver for me too, I suppose. I'm curious about what makes people tick, and I like the idea that I can help them."

"Help them how?"

"Some people just seem to be stuck," she answers. "Stuck in some childhood trauma or some bad habit or some unhappy life. I like the idea that I can get them unstuck. That was actually what I found so interesting about the navigation stuff we did today."

She abruptly stops talking and seems to be thinking about her response. I notice over her shoulder that the sun has completely set. I turn to look through a salty window into the salon and see people, including Jason and Mark, clearing dishes from their tables. Did I miss dinner? How long have I been sitting here? Why am I not even hungry? I turn back to look at Olivia, who has shifted again, and is now sitting a couple feet away from me.

"Is there more to that?" I ask, growing impatient with the pregnant pause.

"More to what?" she asks.

"You were talking about navigation."

"Oh, well, I just mean learning how to navigate through the unknown...how to find your way back...how to keep from getting lost in the first place."

Mark joins us on the bow. I assume he's trying to catch a last glimpse of the sunset as he peers off to the west. There is nothing but darkness over the water, although the stars are beginning to appear in the western sky.

"She's been trying to get me *unstuck* for years," he says, pointing at Olivia.

How in the world did he know we had been talking about getting people unstuck?

"Don't look so surprised, Morgan...I don't hear *magical* voices like you do. I could hear you two through the open window around the corner there," he says, motioning to the port side of the salon where he had eaten dinner with Jason. I notice the crew has opened most of the windows in the salon to welcome in the cool breeze. Jason is nowhere to be seen, and I assume he's gone to his bunk.

Olivia and Jason had struggled with the navigation drills we had done earlier in the day, missing the return mark several times before finally completing the square course successfully. They had trouble following the compass, counting their kick cycles, and controlling their breathing and buoyancy all at the same time. This is not at all unusual with divers who are first learning navigation, especially when they have not yet mastered the first two steps of breath control and neutral buoyancy. Mark had done surprisingly well technically, but he left his children behind in the process.

I could see why Olivia was helping Mark get *unstuck*. He had been living a *successful* life with a growing career and what he thought was a good family and marriage. His life had all the appearances of moving forward, while his most important relationships were stuck and falling apart as he concentrated too much on his goals. Then it all exploded in divorce, and now he couldn't figure out how to move forward.

Mark gives up scanning for the sunset and plops down on the bench between me and Olivia. The three of us sit silently, staring at the water. We're together on the deck, but each of us has wandered off mentally.

As I watch the journey of transformation happen in people's lives around me, I often forget I too am on a growth journey. But I only see it when I look back at my life. I'm never aware of it when it's happening, and I'd like to be. I can see where I was and see where I am now, and good or bad, a lot of me has changed.

But how do I become more aware of the transformation happening to me without once again becoming completely self-absorbed? When I look back at the most transformational events in my life, the biggest changes occurred when I became totally involved in other people's lives. Maybe that was the secret. When I got married, my life was no longer just my own. I now had to consider how my life affected someone else's life if I was to have a successful relationship. I also immediately became a father to Mary's two young children when we said "I do." Everything I thought I knew about myself had to be tossed away. I had no idea how selfish I was until I was forced to share everything with the children now running around my house.

"What's on the agenda tomorrow?" Jason asks as he walks up behind me from the starboard side.

"I thought you went to bed?" I respond, a bit startled by his sudden appearance.

"Nah...I was just talking to some guys out on the dive deck."

"The deep dive," I say in response to his earlier question.

"What's the deep dive?" Mark asks, looking away from the water and back at me. The reluctant tone has returned to his voice.

"A dive reaching depths between sixty and a hundred feet," I answer. "And we'll be hitting the hundred-foot mark tomorrow. I always like to say *real* diving starts at one hundred feet deep."

"Why's that?" Jason asks.

"So, diving less than one hundred feet deep isn't *real* diving?" Olivia asks somewhat sarcastically.

"Ok, *real* is probably the wrong word," I respond. "It's all *real* diving...I just mean to say that the priorities and risks significantly change starting at about a hundred feet. You can no longer just think primarily about your air consumption...no-decompression limits become the most pressing issue." I pause, considering how far I want to delve into this right now.

"And?" Olivia asks, extending the palm of her hand toward me.

"And...I think that's enough for tonight. We'll go over all of this in the morning before the dive. Right now, I'm tired," I say, rising to leave. "Good night. See you all in the morning."

They each respond with a "good night" and remain on the bow as I make my way off to my bunk.

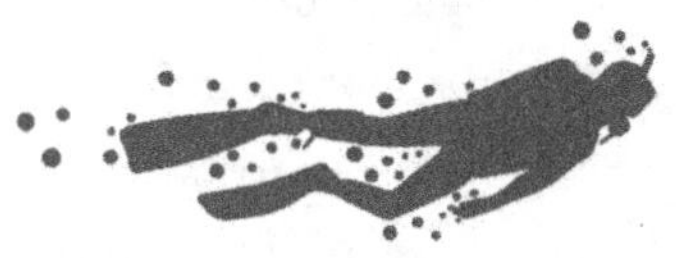

12

"When grace rules your life, you come into a place of abundance."

"What?" is all I say as I prop myself up in my bunk and shake the cobwebs from my head. There's no response. I assume it's the voice again, starting off this sixth day onboard with another riddle of the day. I notice the curtain on my bunk is partially open, which is why the light from the salon above seems so bright. As I fully come to, I realize the voice is in full volume this morning. So strange; I can hear it so clearly, but no one else ever seems to hear it.

I get up slowly and go through my regular morning routine before taking a seat in the galley area, where I watch the chef, Julia, and her assistant put the final touches on breakfast. It appears to be some sort of egg casserole, and it smells delicious. I'm really hungry this morning. My grumbling stomach reminds me that I never ate dinner last night. I'm the first in line at the buffet after the chef motions to me that they're open for business. Jason, Olivia, and Mark emerge from the bunkroom and join me in line.

"Good morning!" I say to the three of them a bit too enthusiastically.

"Good morning," Oliva says in return. Mark and Jason silently raise their eyebrows in my general direction.

We gather our breakfast and return to the table where we always sit. There are no assigned tables, but I watch as all of the other divers return to the same tables they seem to have sat at throughout this journey. We eat in relative silence until I decide to jump into my pre-dive briefing.

"As I've told you before, no-decompression limits are the amount of time a diver can spend at any given depth and still be able to return directly to the surface," I start in. I notice no one is looking at me as I talk.

"You all awake?" I ask. They all look my way and nod, so I continue. "I've taught you from day one to monitor the air supply in your tanks. I ask you over and over again how much air you have in your tanks. I'm trying to get you into the habit of looking at your gauge so often that you can probably guess the pressure left in your tanks at any given time without even stopping to look. I also ask you to indicate your current depth and the amount of time we've been diving. When we move into the advanced open water course, especially on the deep dive, I shift the time question from, 'how long have we been diving?' to, 'how much longer can we remain at this depth without having to decompress?'"

I pause to see if I still have their attention. They're all still looking at me, so I continue.

"I said last night that diving starts at a hundred feet deep because at that depth, the no-decompression limit will almost certainly occur before you run low on air. But the way you monitor your air supply must also change because you have to factor in how much air you will need to make a slow and much longer ascent to the surface, including your precautionary safety stop. Including the three-minute stop, it should take at least six to seven minutes to reach the surface."

Silence follows my little speech. I still can't tell if they're really listening or even awake, for that matter. They all appear to be deep in thought. Maybe they're just tired.

"That reminds me of something you said before," Jason finally says.

"What's that?" I ask. He's definitely awake.

"About transformation," he responds. "You said learning to dive is like a mini-seminar on transformation. A lot of change happens as people move from being scared to breathe underwater to being full-blown divers. That seems like a pretty big transformation, but 'thinking like a diver,' as you say, is a continuation of that process."

He's definitely lost me, and I can tell by Mark and Olivia's scrunched faces that they are lost as well. I resist the urge to ask Jason to clarify what he means and instead attempt to bring his comment back to where I was going with this briefing.

"You are correct," I say. "Like the PADI manual says, thinking like a diver starts with 'Every dive's primary objective is for all divers to return safely. When divers forget this primary objective, significant problems can result.' That's thinking like a diver." Jason is staring at me with a blank expression, so I decide to go back to this comment. "But I'm not sure how that connects with the transformation of a diver?" I ask him.

Jason doesn't respond, but he is nodding his head and seems to know where I'm going with all of this, even if I don't. I decide not to press him again and return to my briefing.

"Let me back up a minute," I say. "I've taught you that breath control is the secret to diving. Breathing in slowly and deeply supplies the body with oxygen, and breathing out deeply removes carbon dioxide from the airways. That process keeps the diver relaxed and thinking clearly. Proper breathing also helps to control buoyancy. I don't ever want you to forget those things, but now I want to build on those skills to grow you as a diver.

"Just to repeat, the primary objective of every dive is to return safely, which starts with breathing. But as you go deeper, you must also pay attention to no-decompression limits to stay safe. Once air supply monitoring and measuring dive times become more routine, you can then add more objectives to your dives...navigating accurately, diving deeper, exploring wrecks, looking for specific fish, photography, et cetera, et cetera...and one of the big secondary objectives is looking out for other divers. As you grow as a diver, you can then turn your thoughts to others around you. You can never forget the primary objective of keeping yourself safe, but you can add the safety of others to your plan as your confidence grows."

"The primary objective in life is survival," Jason says. "But once that is relatively secure, there can be many secondary objectives."

We all turn and look at Jason. He's talking to us, but it feels more like we're watching him talk to himself. He catches himself and looks each of us in the eyes, one by one. We sit patiently, waiting for some sort of explanation.

"The purpose of trials in this life is to move me beyond the primary objective and onto the secondary objectives," Jason explains. "I must become proficient in breathing (life) and buoyancy control (balance) before I can tackle the secondary objective (other people placed in my life). I've been such a mess since Matty died that I can't possibly be much help to other people. My world has gotten so small since that happened."

His description leads me back to my son's death and nearly losing my family and myself as loss and depression consumed all of us. It is not a fate I would wish upon anyone. There have been people throughout my life I have truly not liked, maybe even hated to some degree, and still, I would not wish upon them the loss of a child. Losing a child, a brother, a spouse, a close friend are all transformational events. They change who you are and the way you do life.

Those events may leave you walking with a limp, but ultimately, each of us has to choose if that change will be for better or worse. The key to benefiting from transformation, then, is not so much about focusing on the events taking place in my life but my response to the events taking place in my life.

Why had I never thought about this before? Was it possible to still live an abundant life after losing my son? Was it possible to still experience joy and love and real happiness? I became angry when Mark panicked and bolted for the surface. But my anger was really a hold-over from my own circumstance, not with him. I too was attempting to scratch my way back to the surface of my life, just trying to breathe and maybe risking injury to myself in the process by simply reacting to my new situation instead of thoughtfully considering what to do next. In the moment of my son's death, I no longer wanted to experience joy, even if that was possible. I wanted my life to end sooner rather than later. I don't know if I was ever bold enough to die by suicide, but death had become a welcomed friend. I was subconsciously killing myself. And even if I wasn't going to physically die soon, I would become part of the walking dead...a zombie of sorts who kept moving through life but never really experiencing anything or anyone. Dead but alive. Now that I was thinking again, and not just reacting, how would I rejoin the living?

The voice says, "Look on the deep dive. Be aware. I want to give you something for your future."

"Morgan...Morgan," Olivia says. "Did we lose you there?"

"Oh, sorry," I respond, "Let me explain the deep dive."

I lay out the plan for our dive. We would move along the line that was tied from the boat to a mooring buoy, then down the mooring line that was permanently tied into the *Naked Lady* wreck below. The sandy bottom around the wreck is about one hundred and ten feet deep, ten feet deeper than our target depth of a hundred feet. This was a test. I told the three of them not to exceed a hundred feet deep, which would test their buoyancy control at depth. The bottom at one hundred and ten feet would keep them from getting dangerously deep but would still present a buoyancy challenge to stay off the bottom. We would start with 3,000 psi in our tanks. When one of us got down to 2,000 psi, we would work our way back toward the mooring line. If we did this correctly, we should be in sight of the mooring line with 1,000 psi left in our tanks. We would hit the hundred-foot mark early in the dive, then spiral our way around the wreck as we slowly got shallower to stay well within the no-decompression limit.

I ask them to keep checking each other's tank pressure and no-decompression limits. We would begin our ascent when one of us either reached 800 psi or the two-minute no-decompression limit, which should put us all back on the boat with at least 500 psi in reserve after the ascent and safety stop.

We jump off the boat and make our way to the bow. After checking with each other, I give the thumbs-down signal, and we begin our descent down the mooring line. The current is very light today, and there is at least fifty feet of visibility. As we descend, the sixty-foot wreck of a sailboat emerges from the gloom. It is covered with life. Schools of small bait fish are chased by larger fish known by Hawaiians as Ulua, a type of trevally. A reef shark rests on the deck. A manta ray lazily wings by.

The wreck sits just over a half mile from the Kailua pier in sparkling clear water. No one knows the name of the wreck for certain, but it got the name *Naked Lady* from the story surrounding its sinking. As the legend goes, the owner anchored her sailboat in Kailua Bay and had somehow come to believe her vessel was "infested with little green men." *Of course*, the only way to rid her boat of the little men was with fire. She set fire to the boat, which ended in sinking the vessel and her jumping into the water. She made it to shore, but with no clothes left on her body. Hence, the *Naked Lady*.

As we fin around the wreck, I hear a curious whirring sound in the water. I turn my head to see where the hum is coming from and see the Atlantis submarine, packed with curious tourists, motoring by the wreck. We wave to the children who are pressing their noses to the windows of the sub, and they wave back. There is a commonality to our scuba diving experience and the experience of the people in the submarine, better classified as a submersible. But there is also a big difference. The experience and safety of those in the submersible are being controlled by someone else. As a diver, my experience and safety are controlled by me. They are *near* the water. I am *in* it. They are *observing* an environment. I am *in* an environment.

I watch my students gaze at the schools of fish and the submarine. Do I want to stay in the submarine observing life or do I really want to dive back in since losing my son? I am not the person I was before. But I have a choice whether to just get through life or actually live it. There is an abundance of life still all around me...my remaining family...close friends who love me...generations to come...but do I want to swim in it?

I motion to get my students floating in a tight circle and show them a small slate with all the colors of the spectrum printed on it. The colors appear gray or a dark shade of blue as most of the light waves are filtered out by the depths. I shine my light on the slate to show them how the colors become vivid once again when white light is reintroduced. I also pull a small foam block from my BC pocket to show them how the water pressure at depth has compressed the small air spaces in the foam and completely flattened it.

Mark signals to me he has reached 2,000 psi. Jason and Olivia are still at about 2,300. I motion for them to follow me, and we slowly circle back toward the mooring line. Mark reaches 1,000 psi on his gauge as we finally near the line several minutes later. We take one last look around at the schools of bright yellow snappers flowing over the deck in a wave, then slowly ascend back up the mooring line, make our safety stop, and surface. Back on deck, we wriggle out of our scuba kits and peel off our wetsuits.

"So that was the deep dive?" Mark asks with a smile on his face.

"That was it," I reply.

"That was actually the easiest dive we've made," he says, still smiling. "I'll be honest, I thought that whole thing was gonna freak me out or something. It was actually pretty relaxing. Watching all those fish sweeping over the deck of that wreck is mesmerizing."

"Let's go up to the sun deck and do a little de-brief on that dive," I say. "Bring your logbooks or your phones with the log app with you." We climb the ladder to the upper deck and grab some seats in the shade of the wheelhouse.

"It's a lot easier to control your buoyancy on a deeper dive and just generally easier to dive," I say. "A lot of students freak out at the idea of diving to a hundred feet, but the volume changes in air spaces at depth are less noticeable than they are near the surface, so you don't have to adjust your BC or equalize your ears as often. You also don't feel the effect of the surface waves so much down there. There just seems to be a better rhythm to diving when you get a bit deeper."

"There's a weird sort of peace down there," Jason says.

"Agreed," I reply. "I always find serenity at depth. Even on windy days, when the boat and divers floating at the surface are being tossed around, I find peace on the bottom. As Mark said, the abundance of life at depth can be 'mesmerizing.'"

We go over the details of the dive and log the information into our phone dive apps...depth, time, temperatures, air usage, and so on. We don't get any cell reception on the boat, but the Bluetooth connection between our dive computers and log apps on our phones works just fine. Mark writes the details in his paper logbook.

"I'm gonna shower off," Mark says as he stands and starts to walk toward the ladder. He turns back. "Anyone want to join me for a snack?"

"I'll meet you inside," Jason says as he too stands and walks away.

Olivia remains on the sun deck but moves about fifteen feet aft near the rail hanging over the dive deck to watch the divers below as they climb back onto the swim step. I decide to stay in the shade.

I'm mulling over this idea of an abundant life. Was Jesus the example of an abundant life? Afterall, he said, "I came that they may have life, and have it abundantly." But he didn't possess much as far as money or earthly things were concerned, religious officials were constantly plotting to kill him, and his life ended in one of the most brutal forms of capital punishment ever invented. Even what he considered to be his *ministry* only lasted about three turbulent years. I get the idea of an abundant life after death in some sort of eternity, but what about abundance in the tumultuous life I was living now?

I often find peace on the other side of turmoil, but not in the middle of it. I go through tumultuous events or circumstances, then somehow find solace on the other side. I've never enjoyed the often-painful process of transformation, but it always produces something new, even exciting, if I just remain on the journey. It reminds me of pushing through the hassles of donning scuba gear, shuffling over a boat deck, or trudging down the sandy beach, contending with the waves, then plunging below the surface. I never experience the abundance of life—joy in simple moments with family, a fantastic adventure with Mary, winning a hard-fought victory—if I'm not willing to push through the waves of inconvenience, travel delays and flight cancellations, and ultimately loss.

I notice a smile on Olivia's face as she watches the crew below help divers who are struggling to get back onto the swim step. She is trying to get her father to change...get him "unstuck," as he put it.

I'm trying to modify his behavior as well. I'm trying to turn him into a diver. The truth is I can never actually make him a diver. I can show him the steps, but he has to make the decision to become a diver. On the deep dive, I decided to back off a bit and let him explore his own abilities. I was there if he needed me, but I wasn't directing his every action.

I have tried to control people in my life when I believe they are doing the wrong thing. My success rate is not good. For starters, when I think someone is doing the "wrong thing," I've already placed myself in a position of judgment. I believe I know something they don't know. Even if that's true, that doesn't mean I get to sit in judgment over them.

Carlos comes to mind. I had decided he was one of those instructors who talks too much and categorized him based on a couple of short encounters. I also had often caught myself lecturing Mary on ways we could better handle things in our relationship, which had been devastated by loss. I had placed myself outside of the church, deciding that most people in the church were too judgmental, not even seeing the hypocrisy in my opinion of them.

"What are you thinking about?" Olivia calls out to me, interrupting my train of thought. She's staring at me from across the small sundeck. She stands and walks over to sit down in the chair beside me.

"I'm wondering how I know when I'm influencing and loving someone versus judging and trying to control them." I pause and stare off at the shore. I can see the distinct shape of Royal Kona Resort peeking out from around the boat's wheelhouse off the starboard bow. I remember sitting in the hotel bar there along the water's edge, sipping a Mai Tai, and watching the sunset. It seems so *touristy*, and I don't know why I love that place so much. I think it's the long outdoor corridor that leads to the front desk that is lined with portraits of the kings and queens who have ruled Hawaii over the years.

The Big Island was once the capital of this remote atoll after King Kamehameha united all of the islands under his leadership in 1795. Eventually, the capital was moved to Maui, then to Oahu. Hawaii is also the *youngest* of the islands, still growing through violent volcanic activity, constantly being transformed. There is such a rich cultural history in these islands...a culture that was pretty much wiped out by overzealous missionaries who seemed far more interested in behavior modification (judgment and control) than sharing the way of Jesus (love and influence).

"Are you going to finish that thought?" Olivia persists.

"What thought?" I ask.

"How do you know when you're influencing and loving someone versus just judging and controlling?" she responds.

"There is a willingness on my part to actually enter into life with the other person and walk with them to a conclusion that is neither mine nor their own," I say. "I'm just realizing that's how I know. I mean, what would happen if I simply listened to Mary and walked with her through her grief instead of thinking I know what she needs to hear or do? I'm not her answer, but maybe I can walk with her to an answer. Maybe that's abundant life."

"I think I'm following you," she says, but her tone says otherwise.

"When I approach someone humbly because I see hurt or pain in their life," I continue, "I have to stop myself from jumping to the conclusion I know what they need, even when I've suffered through similar circumstances and I am convinced I have the answer. Jesus teaches to abandon my agenda and set my conclusions aside so I can walk with a person to the *real* destination God has already established...by the way, it's always something different and far better than either of us anticipated."

"And, again, how does Jesus fit into all of this?" she asks.

"I was just thinking, if anyone had all the answers, it was him," I answer. "But he constantly taught about just loving people instead of judging them. When I begin to live out this principle of laying aside judgment no matter how 'sure' I am about having the answer for someone else, I begin to move into a lifestyle of grace. And a lifestyle of grace is the only path to answer the *why* questions of life."

"The *why* questions," she repeats.

I stand and start pacing as I process aloud.

"Many people in my life have told me over the years, 'Don't ever ask why.' But I've never bought that answer...I've always asked why. Since the day my son died, I've asked even more. I'm never satisfied with the answers people give me, like, 'That's just how it works' or 'We can never understand God's ways' or 'Everything happens for a reason.' I think God answers the why questions...Jesus always seems to be answering the why questions for his followers. I want an open door...I want to know why."

I stop pacing and look at Olivia as I drop back into my seat. My shoulders slump. I notice my pulse throbbing in my ears. My heart rate is elevated. I don't know if I'm making any sense. Olivia just stares at me as if she's waiting for me to catch my breath.

"You asked me last night, 'What's the secret to life?'" I say. "Obviously, I don't know completely, but I think the secret to an *abundant* life is to continue asking the *why* question until I get a satisfying answer. This is the journey. I continue to seek God, always asking why, so I can learn. This changes my job a lot. Instead of judging people's behavior, assuming I already know what they should do or not do, I instead enter into their journey with them, encouraging them to keep asking the *why* questions that have led them to where they are in life. When the *why* questions start getting answered in your life, the abundance is almost too much to bear. It's a revelation!"

"So, what's *your* answer?" Olivia asks.

"My answer to what?" I ask.

"Why did your son have to die?"

"I don't know yet," I answer.

"Can I pray over you?" she asks.

"Can you what?"

"Can I pray over you?" she repeats.

I look at her and don't respond. I think I know what she means, but I'm not sure. I notice she asked if she could pray *over* me, instead of pray *for* me. I have had people ask or even tell me they would pray *for* me, but I never had anyone ask if they could pray *over* me.

"It's this thing I do," she says. "I pray *over* you as a way to enter into whatever's going on in your life, as opposed to praying *for* you, which keeps me more at a distance from the issue you're concerned about."

"Um...sure...I guess," I say.

"Can I put my hand on your shoulder?" she asks.

I find the question odd since she's not exactly shy about touching people. Before I can answer, she stands up and places her right hand on my shoulder. She opens her other hand to the heavens, palm up, facing the sky like a satellite dish. I'm not sure what to expect, but I can already physically feel a sort of electricity passing through her hand into my shoulder and radiating throughout my body.

"You're a father...you know that, right?" she asks. Her eyes are wide open. She's looking at me...she's looking *into* me, actually. "You know you're still a dad, even since your son died...right?" she asks.

"Yeah...I guess I do," I answer weakly.

"No...look at me...like you need to get this. God made you a father. It's your identity. You have a very strong anointing on your life to be a father."

I look up at her. Her eyes are clear, but mine begin to blur with tears. I think I know what she means by "anointing," like some sort of calling in my life. Other people have said this to me, but never with the intensity that Olivia is saying it.

"You need to get this," she repeats. "God…show him."

I close my eyes, and a movie starts playing. I can see my son James about twenty feet under crystal blue water. His older brother Ben appears and struggles desperately to bring him to the surface. Ben loses his grip on top of the waves, and my youngest closes his eyes and drifts back into the deep. The scene shifts, and I see myself on a boat going back to Catalina Island a day or two after we had given up the search for my missing son. I can clearly see the spot off China Point where he drowned. The GPS coordinates appear in my mind: 33° 19.424' N, 118° 29.033' W. The words appear, "Last Known Position."

The scene shifts again, and I'm now driving my older son's tiny Boston Whaler boat back to the mainland. Wind is whipping salt water into my face, and I'm shouting to the heavens. "Why, God, why? Why did you take my son?" This goes on for hours, and I hear nothing in answer but the wind. Then there is silence like someone has pressed mute on the remote control. I hear nothing.

"I know something about losing a son," I then hear all around me. This can't be the voice of God because it's not a real answer to my question. But I'm not really asking a question…I'm demanding that God fix my problem. This isn't a request, and he doesn't really answer my question…just "I know something about losing a son."

I feel like I'm lapsing in and out of consciousness as Olivia continues to pray, and I can't make out what she's saying. It sounds like a language I've never heard before. The experience is a trip through time more than what I would consider a prayer. Maybe this is what prayer is supposed to be…a shared journey instead of a laundry list of things I'd like God to take care of for me. I hear another voice with a very different tone.

"You're not really a father," it snarls. "You couldn't even keep your own son safe, so I took him like I told Mary I would."

"Is that you? Did you take my son?" I call out to God.

"I did not take your son," the voice replies. "You have an enemy, and he took your son."

"But you could have stopped him!" I shout.

"I know something about losing a son," he says.

She stops praying. I'm not completely sure what all she said, but there are now three more people sitting around me, and they all have their hands on my shoulders. Two of them are openly weeping, and so am I. I look into each of their faces. I see Jason and Olivia, but don't know the other two women other than seeing them around on the boat. Wait...no. Now I think one of them is the chef, Julia. They've come out of nowhere to join in this prayer *over* me. I am wrecked, but so alive.

"How do you feel?" Olivia asks.

"Clean," I say. "Like I just stepped out of the shower. I also feel like something has dropped off me. I feel lighter and more alive... alive like I'm ready to go do something."

"There is," she says with a smile. "And you're already doing it, you just don't know it yet."

"Teaching scuba?" I ask, not sure why that was the first thing to pop into my mind. "Being a scuba instructor doesn't seem very God-like if you ask me."

"You're teaching more than just scuba," she responds. "You just don't see it as that. You've changed a lot of people's lives, based on the stories you tell. But you're naturally gifted at it, so you don't see it."

"That doesn't make sense," I say.

"When people are gifted at something, they don't see it as special. It just seems normal to them. But to other people who aren't gifted in that particular way, it seems extraordinary."

"Some instructor I am…I feel like you're instructing me," I reply.

"I'm taking the journey with you, just like you described about an hour ago. Instead of trying to figure you out…you called it 'judging'…I just chose in this moment to make myself vulnerable just like you did, and Jason did, and Bob here did." She points to the chef.

"I thought your name was Julia?" I say to Bob.

"No, Julia's my sous chef," Bob responds. "You've seen her helping me in the galley."

I now wonder how she got the name Bob, why I didn't know that was her name, and why I never thought it was worth the time to learn Julia's name. Olivia, it seems, knows everyone's names.

"And then Andrea joined us," Olivia says, pointing toward the other woman in our impromptu little group. "And God filled the space."

There are no real words to describe what just happened, so none of us try. We sit for a moment in silence, which is broken by an announcement from the captain that we will shortly be pulling the anchor and heading to a new spot off the island. Dinner will be served while we're underway. The chef hurries back to her galley. I head to the shower and a change of clothes. Dinner is fresh fish with rice pilaf, and the mood is light. I feel a new energy on our boat, and I feel light. A heavy burden was lifted off me today, and I feel like a new, better-fitting yolk was placed on my shoulders…there is still a burden, but it seems lighter and makes sense somehow. It is a burden of fatherhood that I owe the people around me. It is true fatherhood that seeks to lift others up, not dictate down to them. It is well-fitted and comfortable. I will gladly bear it.

Later in the evening, I say my goodnights and head to the bunks below. I drift off to sleep thinking about what happened to me today…thinking about how people I didn't even know joined into a moment to pray for me and the tangible feeling it left in my soul.

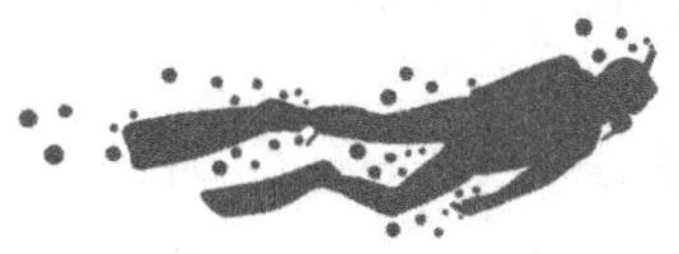

13

I awake early on day seven to a glowing waterfall of sun cascading down the stairway. The sight should lift my spirits, but instead, I feel darkness. There's a depression in my soul that is contrary to the lightness I felt last night. I'm where I want to be at the moment and doing what I want to do. My students are making good progress and starting to look like seasoned divers.

So, what's wrong with me? Is the feeling I have some sort of chemical imbalance in my brain...some sort of low-blood-sugar depression? I get out of my bunk and get ready for the day. I think coffee and a bagel may lift my low feeling. They do not.

I'm sitting at a table in the galley area, looking through the logs on my dive computer. I look up and see Carlos, the other instructor, sitting on the other side of the salon. There has been no sense of camaraderie between us since that day at the beach. I still don't like him, and I'm pretty sure he doesn't like me. Olivia emerges from the stairway to the bunkroom and makes her way over to the galley for a cup of coffee. She says good morning to Carlos, then makes her way over to sit at my table. I don't like that she gets along with him.

"You still pissed at that guy?" Olivia asks, tilting her head toward Carlos, who is now engaged with his students at their table.

"I suppose...I'm not really sure why he bugs me so much," I answer.

"I know why," she says, her ever-present smile right on cue. "It was that day at the beach when we did the buoyancy checks and he was yelling at my dad. You don't like other people interfering with your teaching process. You have a pretty different style than he does... same with that other instructor I saw in the pool before we came out on this little cruise. They hover over their students, intent on preventing mistakes. You, on the other hand, embrace mistakes in a weird sort of way."

"True," I say. "It's the way I learn, so I assume other people learn that way too."

"We do. But we probably learn the other way too. I've watched the other instructors. You're right, they don't teach like you do, but their students seem to learn. Why do you get so hung up on that stuff? Why do you care what other instructors do or think?"

"Hmm...good question," I respond. "I never really understood why people grieve differently either."

"I'm guessing we're not talking about teaching styles anymore," she says. "Does this have something to do with me praying over you yesterday?"

"Oh...sorry...just feeling a little depressed this morning, and the coffee doesn't seem to be working. I appreciate what you did for me, but it kind of feels like I came down this morning after some sort of high last night. Ever since I lost James, anytime I feel even a little depressed, I wonder if I'm still grieving and spiral into a hole. Around the time he died, my wife Mary and I knew some other couples who lost their sons. We all had very different ways of grieving. One couple split up, but I think they had problems before they lost their son. Tragedy amplifies anything that's already going on in your life. Tragedy and grief strip you of your defenses. All the little tricks you play in your mind to avoid confronting problems...well, you just lose the energy to play those tricks anymore. You collapse into your actual life instead of the life you constantly try to convince yourself you are living."

"You ever think about writing a book?" she asks.

"A what? Did you just tell me to write a book? Are you serious?"

"Yes, I am," she answers. She looks serious, but she's still smiling. "I've just never really talked to anyone like you before. You have all this stuff inside. Some of it's pretty fucked up, but some of it is spot on. It's like you fade in and out of some of the most profound things I've ever heard and some of the most broken thinking I've ever encountered."

"Why do you swear so much?" I ask.

"Why don't you swear at all?" she asks in return.

"I asked first."

"I don't know," she says. "My church friends always ask me to stop. They can't really seem to figure me out at all. I love Jesus and I love the church...I just love people in general. But all the people in my church family mostly seem interested in getting me to stop swearing...oh, that and give up the lesbian thing. They don't get that either. I had an older guy tell me once that I would make such a great Christian if I could clean up my mouth and find a nice man to marry."

"Did you punch him in the face?" I ask.

"No," she says with a laugh. "It just made me love him more. I love when people feel like they can be honest with me, even if we totally disagree. Kinda like you and that other instructor. Like I asked before, why does he bug you so much?"

"I've been sitting here most of the morning trying to figure that out," I reply.

"Oh, but you can't get out of that swearing question first," she says. "I noticed right away that you don't really ever swear, but I heard you say something under your breath once that sounded a lot like swearing. I think you secretly swear to yourself, but not out loud, which is kinda weird, actually."

"I wasn't raised around people who cursed, drank, or smoked, so I guess it got drilled into me somehow that that's not the way to behave."

"Yes, but you drink, and I know you swear in your head. Do you smoke?"

"No," I respond. "I tried it as a kid and got so sick that I never tried it again. Same with the drinking. I never had the fortitude to remain a big-time drinker. There was a decade in my twenties where I tried out the drunk lifestyle, but it always made me so sick that I couldn't stick with it. It was too debilitating. And weed and drugs just never interested me."

"It's like you've been preserved or something," she says.

"What do you mean, *preserved*?"

"Like there's some specific purpose for your life and, no matter how hard you try to mess it up, you're not allowed to walk outside of it. You try to walk another way, excessive drinking being the best example, but you always get turned back around by something or someone. You can't seem to get out of this purpose."

I'm staring at her now as she once again lays my soul bare. Olivia has a way of making me feel so exposed and understood at the same time. She's good at this.

"And gambling," I say.

"Gambling?"

"There was a period where I spent a lot of time in casinos until one day, I just stopped. I just lost interest...good thing too because I really was starting to have a problem. It's funny you say that about being protected or preserved though," I say.

"Funny how?" she asks.

"It just reminds me of a time a coworker got me so drunk in New Orleans that he talked me into visiting a strip club," I respond. "He knew I wasn't into that sort of thing, so he made it his mission to get me into one. I don't remember much about that night, but he said as one of the girls approached me, it looked like someone or something reached out of the dark, grabbed me by the collar, pulled me out the door, and led me away down the street to my hotel. He said I was pulled so quickly down the sidewalk that he couldn't even catch up."

"So, I'm right, aren't I?" It's more of a statement than a question. "I finally figured you out, and that scares the shit out of you."

"Again with the swearing," I respond.

"Would you get over the fucking swearing thing already? You just told me you went to a strip club," she says. "Why is swearing such a big hangup for you? You probably keep track of who's swearing, how many times they swore in the last few hours...you probably know exactly who's drinking what and exactly how much in any social situation. You know who smokes and who doesn't, no matter how much they try to hide it. You know exactly who's gay and who isn't. Who cheats, who doesn't. You keep track of everything like some sort of scoreboard. You don't come across as judgmental, but you're constantly judging everyone. Aren't you?"

"Maybe," I mutter.

"You just don't say it out loud, so no one knows," she continues. There's a playful tone in her voice, but a serious note as well. "I'm on to you, Morgan. It even bothers you that I'm gay, but there's something you love about me at the same time. You hold all this tension in your head, and you never really know where to land on any subject. You're shockingly open-minded and judgmental all at the same time. You're crazy, but you're also fascinating. That's why I said you should write a book. Maybe it would help you sort all this stuff out."

This woman seems like she knows me better than I know myself. I mull over what she's saying and wonder how she could have deduced so much in such a short time. When she talks, I feel like she is verbalizing what I'm thinking. Does she do this with everyone? I feel a sort of intimacy with her, but not in any sexual way...more like a kinship...like we're related even though we're not. She's nothing like me, but she seems to process information in a very similar manner to me. I try to shrug off the feeling, telling myself she's just a good therapist, but it won't go away.

"So, what about that other instructor?" she asks.

"What about him?" I ask in return.

"Why does he bug you so much?"

"I'm honestly trying to figure that out," I say. "I wonder if I think the way I teach is somehow more advanced or just flat-out better? I mean...obviously I do, but why do I care what he does?"

"Because you love his students too," she says.

"Because...I love...his students... too," I repeat slowly. "Well, it's true that there are few things I love more than people who want to learn. So, I guess I love students in general. I love anyone open to learning new things. I'm naturally drawn to people who are curious like I am."

"And you want to see his students learn just as much as we are," she says. "You are a good teacher, but you already know that. Your hang-up is other teachers. You think you're a *better* teacher than they are instead of just a *different* teacher than they are."

For the gate is narrow and the way is constricted that leads to life, and there are few who find it. Jesus's words float through my brain. I feel like I've found the *narrow gate* to real life, but I can't seem to enter through it. I've conformed myself to a non-judgmental lifestyle outwardly, but I can't seem to get there inwardly.

"I heard a sermon once about human trafficking," I say to Olivia.

"This preacher talked about the battles to free boys and girls caught in the depths, the depravity, and the inhumanity of the sex trade. But instead of the usual focus on the heroes, who make daring rescues of those trapped in this horrible trade, he asked who's reaching out to the criminals who kidnap people into slavery and those men who pay for sex with young girls? I remember thinking as I listened, 'wait a minute, reach out to the horrible people who perpetuate these crimes?' He explained that to break this cycle, we would have to understand that Jesus called us to a universal love that knows *no bounds* and applies to everyone—good people and bad people, however you define them."

"Sounds like what Jesus taught," she says. "Correct, but sorta impossible."

"I supposedly subscribe to this idea of love that knows no bounds, but I can't even get close to the idea of loving these perpetrators. Hell, I can't even get myself to like and respect another instructor just because we disagree a bit about technique."

"Is that a question or a conclusion?" Olivia asks. "By the way, you just said hell, in case you're keeping track of the swearing.

"I agree with you that it sounds a lot like what Jesus taught," I say. "But it looks very little like what most people would call Christianity. Most of the Christianity presented to me throughout my life sounds a lot like *us and them*; like the Christians are the good guys and everyone else are the bad guys."

"Isn't that the transformation you've been talking about?" she asks. "You said true transformation is really unimaginable...it's something that happens to you, and you become something you can't even imagine until it happens."

"I suppose that's true," I say.

"You don't sound so sure anymore," she replies.

I stand up from the table and say, "I'm gonna go talk to Carlos." I walk across the galley area over to his table. He's watching me walk over with a curious look on his face.

"Hi. I'm John Morgan," I say. "Just thought I should *officially* introduce myself."

"Nice to meet you," he says. "Carlos Mendes. I was going to introduce myself to you earlier, but you didn't seem too interested in meeting me."

"Why do you say that?" I ask.

"I don't know for sure...Olivia told me it bothered you when I tried to help your student on the beach the other day."

I look back at Olivia. She's watching the two of us and smiling. I feel like she somehow arranged this little meeting between the two of us instructors. Carlos looks her way with a knowing glance. Now I'm feeling like I got set up...like the two of them had been talking about me and trying to figure out why he bothered me so much. I turn back toward Carlos, not really knowing what to say next.

"Yeah, I don't know," Carlos begins. "It looked like your student, Mark—I think that's his name—was struggling, and he needed some air in his BC. I couldn't tell if you noticed, so instinct just took over and I yelled at him to inflate his BC."

"It was under control," I say a bit too quickly. A flash of anger rises. I smother it. "But I also know sometimes it just *looks* like things aren't under control when I'm teaching. I let them make mistakes, then let them try to figure out a solution. I debrief them later and we try again. It kinda gives me a point of reference when I can say, 'remember what happened last time?' and ask them how they corrected the problem. It takes a lot more time to teach that way, but my students seem more qualified to run their own dives at the end of our course together."

"How'd you come up with that?" he asks.

"By doing it wrong for a bunch of years, then wondering why my students could never seem to remember what I told them," I answer. "I found myself frustrated, always chasing them around fixing all their little mistakes until I assisted another instructor at this shop where I was teaching. I immediately noticed she presented information as questions to her students instead of statements. I also noticed the students seemed much more engaged and remembered more."

"Maybe the students just liked her personality," he offers.

"Probably. She was a very dynamic person. But there was also something to the technique. I tried it myself with my next class, and I found the students repeating things to me as the course moved on."

"But you still have to *tell* them things sometimes, right?"

"Yes, but even then, it can be done in a way that opens them up to asking questions so they feel like you're on the journey with them, as Olivia likes to say. I also let them know when they taught me something. I'm still open to learning too. They *love* that."

"Makes sense," Carlos says. "I have to think it through some more, but there's some good stuff in there."

We talk for about an hour, and the tension between us fades. I began to see him as just another instructor who wants the best for his students. He, like me, is willing to swap any methods and any information that helps himself, his students, or any other instructor.

We conclude our conversation as his students begin to join us, each carrying their breakfast to our table. I excuse myself, walk back across to the galley, and load a plate with pancakes. Mark and Jason have joined Olivia at her table, where they have all begun eating. I carry my pancakes over and sit down with them, still thinking about my conversation with Carlos. I misjudged him. I register how often one little interaction can lead me to put someone in a category of people with whom I don't want to associate. Carlos wasn't the first time.

"What's up for today?" Jason asks as I sit down.

"Wreck dive," I say between bites.

"Wasn't that a wreck dive yesterday?" Mark asks, referring to the *Naked Lady*.

"It was...but the focus of that dive was mostly the depth, not the wreck itself so much. This time we're going to focus more on the wreck itself."

"So, are we going inside of it or something?" Mark asks.

"No," I answer quickly. "There's not much on this wreck to go inside of, per se, but even if there was, we wouldn't be going inside."

"Why not?" Jason asks.

"It can get dangerous real fast inside of a wreck. A few wrong kicks can stir up a silt storm and create zero visibility. Then you have limited time to get out while you can't see your hand in front of your face. There's a whole wreck diving specialty you can be certified in that involves four wreck dives. The last dive includes penetration into the wreck with special equipment and special precautions, but we only do the first wreck dive in the series during the advanced open water class."

"So, if we're not going inside, what are we doing?" Olivia asks.

"On this wreck dive, we will mostly talk about navigating around the wreck safely," I answer, "controlling our buoyancy so we don't stir up any silt, identifying and avoiding any danger spots on the wreck, and finding the mooring line at the end of the dive to get back to the boat."

I brief them on many of the considerations in wreck diving with a special emphasis on safety. I also talk about the reasons we should never attempt to remove any artifacts from a wreck, especially on wrecks of historical significance.

"Let's clean up our dishes and meet on the dive deck," I conclude.

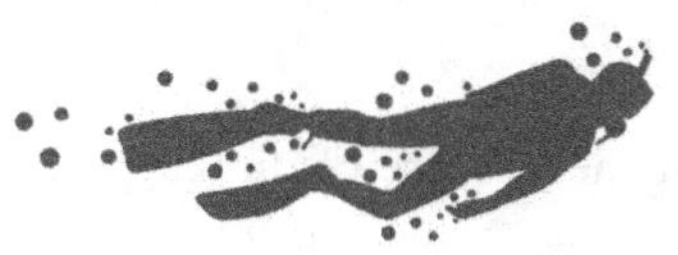

14

"The wreck we will be diving today is nicknamed the *Predator*, which is an old military landing craft," I say as we emerge from the salon onto the dive deck. Mark, Olivia, and Jason follow me to where our gear is staged and begin a few minor adjustments.

"It doesn't have any real historical significance, but it does have a somewhat interesting past," I say. "It sits in about ninety feet of water, so what do we need to be thinking about as we dive?"

"Air consumption," Mark says.

"True, as it is with every dive, but what becomes just as important with deeper dives?" I ask.

"No-decompression limits?" Jason says.

"Are you asking me or telling me?"

"Telling you...it's no-decompression limits," he says more assertively.

"Correct. We'll have to monitor our no-decompression limits carefully, just like we did on the other wreck," I continue. "As with all wrecks, there are a few different stories surrounding the *Predator*, but the most common story is after its use as a military landing craft, it was refitted to handle shark diving cages. You can see the remains of the crane that was likely used to lower and raise the cages. Oh, and you'll see that the engines are still in the hull."

"Didn't you say that wrecks can mess with your compass too?" Mark asks.

"Yes, and your general sense of direction. On our dive, I want you to get a basic understanding of the layout of the wreck," I continue, "and note any currents in the area and how they might differ at the surface compared to the bottom. I also want you to get a general bearing with your compass to determine the direction it is pointing along the bottom from stern to bow. We'll note this direction from above while still on the mooring line, then we'll note the direction again near the wreck to see if the metal of the hull affects our magnetic compasses."

I look past my students and survey the sky. I notice there are no clouds to be seen anywhere. The wind has picked up a bit from the west, and the boat rocks from side to side on the growing swell. We don our wetsuits and slip into the shoulder straps of our BCs. I offer a few last safety precautions about air consumption. We stand and shuffle over to the rail, focusing on our balance on the rocking deck. We don our fins, then, one-by-one, stride off into the water.

Despite the swell, visibility is good today, and I can make out the outline of the wreck instantly as we begin to descend. I stop them about halfway down the mooring line and signal for them to take a reading on their compass to determine the direction the wreck lies along the bottom. We descend farther and take another reading while hovering just off the side of the deck. The metallic structure of the wreck is clearly pulling on the magnetic north needle of our compasses. I spot the other divers from our boat as we all begin to circumnavigate the wreck. We swim past the other group of students, and their instructor Carlos gives me a subtle OK sign. Our conversation earlier has put us at ease with each other in the water, and the seeds of trust have been planted in me.

We spot a few moray eels curiously poking their heads from the wreck as we continue to slowly swim for about forty-five minutes. I note there is a good amount of fishing line adorning the wreck as we swim, and I point it out to my students as a potential danger. Wrecks attract fish and fish attract fishermen. I cut some of the line loose from the wreck with a pair of shears I carry on my kit and coil it up in my hand to take with me so it doesn't entangle any wildlife. I look up from my activity and notice Mark is drifting backward into another, heavier fishing line that is swaying in the current behind him. Olivia and Jason are closer to me and looking in my direction as the other line begins to wrap slowly around the valve of their father's tank. I quickly wrap up the line I am coiling, stuff it in a pocket on my BC, and move around Jason and Olivia toward Mark.

As I approach, he's becoming aware of the line around his tank valve as it begins to restrict his movements. Despite my earlier warnings not to attempt to spin around to locate an entanglement, he begins to slowly spin, wrapping the heavy monofilament line tighter and tighter around his equipment and body. I see his eyes widen as the telltale signs of panic start to cross his face. I give him a signal to remain still so I can remove the line from his gear. Jason signals to me that he has reached our predetermined air pressure to return to the mooring line. Olivia has more air than Jason, but she too is nearing the limit we had set. I indicate they should stay together and begin looking for the mooring line while I unentangle Mark. They don't move and keep pointing at their father, who appears to be struggling harder against the line now enveloping his body and gear.

Carlos appears at my side, pulling out a dive knife and signaling to me he is there to help. I don't see his students anywhere and assume he has already sent them back to the surface. I signal to Carlos to take Olivia and Jason to the surface while I keep working with Mark. They don't appear to want to leave their father, but Carlos gently pulls them back to the mooring line. I continue working with Mark, switching back and forth between cutting the line off his gear and looking him in the eyes to reassure him he will be OK. But I'm beginning to lose eye contact with him as he keeps looking down at his pressure gauge. He has passed our predetermined air pressure limit for returning to the surface and begins tapping rapidly on his gauge. I'm having trouble keeping him in one place as I cut him free.

I wave in his face to get his attention and point to the small reserve tank I have attached to my primary tank. I show him that I also still have quite a bit of air in my primary tank. I try to reassure him we have enough air to return to the surface safely. I have almost freed Mark when Carlos returns with an extra tank and attached regulator as a backup. Mark is now free from the fishing line, and I begin to escort him back to the mooring line. He's a bit hard to control and is trying to swim faster than I let him. Carlos helps me contain Mark as we swim him back to the mooring line, where we begin our slow ascent.

I keep ahold of Mark's dangling pressure gauge to slow his ascent and monitor his remaining air. Mark is still kicking his fins rapidly as we reach the fifteen-foot depth level and attempts to keep moving up the line past the safety stop. I stop him with a gentle yank on his pressure gauge and hold him in place by grasping a strap on his BC. I turn him to look at me as we make the three-minute stop. He finally relents and stops kicking. By the time we surface, he only has about 100 psi in his tank—far lower than we had planned—but he is safe. I let Mark catch his breath before we swim back around to the stern of the dive boat to climb the ladder. We climb onto the boat, walk to our spot on the benches, sit down, and take off our gear. Mark is staring at me. He starts to speak but doesn't seem to know what to say. I try to imagine what he's thinking.

"I'm proud of you," I finally say, putting a hand on his shoulder.

"For what? For getting myself tangled up and freaking out again?" he says.

"No. I'm proud of you for keeping it together down there while I untangled you."

"Are you alright, Dad?" Jason asks as he walks toward us, his wetsuit now pulled down to his waist.

"Yeah, I'm fine," Mark responds, waiving Jason off. Jason looks to me, and I flash him on an OK sign, which doesn't erase the scowl on his face.

"We weren't sure what to do," Jason says. "That started to seem like it could be pretty bad."

"You all handled it well," I respond. "You did what I asked you to, and everyone got out safe."

"I'm glad Carlos was there to take us to the surface," Olivia says as she walks over and sits next to Mark. "I was starting to freak out a little while you were cutting my dad free. You looked at us with that calm look you get in your eyes, and I somehow knew things were under control."

"Yeah, I really appreciated Carlos's help on that one," I say. "It definitely helped having him there."

I reassure Mark again as I peel off my wetsuit. He looks calmer to me, so I head for the indoor showers. I close my eyes as the warm water pours over me, realizing I skipped right past my typical dive debriefing. I think through all the scenarios that could have unfolded underwater. Thanks to some pre-planning and Carlos's help, none of those scenarios materialized. I feel a sense of affection replace the feelings I had earlier toward Carlos. He was legitimately there for us and really helped in what could have turned into a dangerous situation. One simple conversation changed everything between us.

The water continues to pour down my back as an odd chill passes down my spine. I again contemplate what could have played out in the depths. I had seriously wondered as I cut away the line if Mark was going to keep his head on straight. I had many preconceived thoughts upon meeting him and watching him interact with others. I pegged him early on as someone who would likely panic underwater and wondered if I had somehow willed that upon him. He had learned a lot about himself these past few days, as had I, somehow outstepping his demons to become a diver. I didn't have much hope for Mark's diving future with me, just as I had little hope for a relationship with Carlos. At the same time, I held onto the belief that the true fruit of this life is relationships with other people. So why do I so quickly rule out people in my life? How many relationships could have taken a very different turn with one simple conversation?

I climb out of the shower, towel off, and get dressed. I can't seem to collect myself and pass on lunch, which would be an opportune time to debrief the last dive. I head to my bunk, draw the curtain, and lay back in the dark. I need time to process. I have a way of pushing my emotions aside in an urgent situation, such as what happened with Mark that day. This ability allows me to focus on the problem at hand in a logical manner. But my emotional response never really dissipates, it just gets shoved to a moment later when I have time to experience it. Often it surprises me.

James drifts back into my thoughts—drowning of all things. How many people have I saved or prevented from drowning, Mark being the latest example? The bitter irony of losing my son in that exact manner was too much to bear. I lay in the dark and a familiar pain wells up in my rapidly-beating heart as tears begin to roll down the side of my face.

There was a period a few years after my son died that I could not get off the couch other than to go to bed at night. For a week I lay there, day after day, eating very little. I would fade in and out of a sleep state, dreaming and hallucinating. After a few days, I could no longer tell if I was awake or asleep. Mary was worried and not sure what to do for me. I found myself replaying my entire life laying on that couch in severe depression. I had not really allowed myself to grieve, and it built up to the degree that my body started shutting down.

That week was followed by several months of rebuilding my life. I sought out and met with many people who had played significant roles throughout my life. My life had been demolished, and I needed to figure out how to rebuild it. So, I reconstructed my past and imagined a new future. There were many things I could still use from my past life, but I had become a new person…I had been transformed, and I needed a new plan for my life.

I drift back into the present, wondering how many people like Carlos I have judged in my life. I argue with myself that it's just easier to categorize people than it is to consider them as individuals. I had placed Carlos into a category of instructors that I had chosen to dislike. Once I got to know him, he literally came to my rescue. A deeper bond had formed that allowed me to see him as more than just a category. He was a person to me.

Was this the fruit borne from tragedy in my life? Could death really beget life?

I pick up a book to read when I hear, "Fruit is the only evidence of a transformed life." I can no longer read as I contemplate the meaning of that phrase. I lay there in confusion, then finally surrender and go up to the galley area for dinner. I see Mark, Olivia, and Jason sitting together eating. It's prime rib night, and the tables are alive with chatting divers enjoying the feast. There is laughter all around me, and all seem to be in good spirits.

Instead of sitting with my group, I sit with Carlos and his students. I sense his students' bonds with each other and their instructor as they talk. I look across the galley and catch Olivia's eye as she gives me a quick wink. I enjoy listening to how Carlos's students had been progressing this week before they decide to join another group in a board game. As the table empties, I turn to Carlos.

"Hey, I didn't get a chance to thank you earlier, but I really appreciated your help down there today," I say. "Things were starting to get out of hand, and Mark was on the verge of completely freaking out on me."

"Yeah, I was gonna say something to you after that dive, but you kind of vanished," he replies.

"Sorry about that. I had to go clear a few things up in my head," I say.

"It's weird what happened," he says, shrugging off my response. "I had my students back on the boat, and one of them told me it looked like someone had gotten tangled in the fishing line that was all over the wreck. So I grabbed an extra kit the crew had set up on deck and jumped back in. I'm glad we didn't need it."

"Just having you there and prepared brought me a lot of peace of mind. And taking Olivia and Jason to the surface for me was huge."

"You know what, brother...I was just happy to help," he says with a broad grin. "I was hoping to get to know you on this trip. That wasn't exactly how I expected it to happen, but, hey, whatever it took. I've heard about you before and I knew from your reputation you had a different approach than I do to teaching scuba. I'm still finding my teaching style, five years in now, and I was hoping to steal some of your ideas."

"Hey, no secrets here," I reply. "I'm happy to share, and I want to hear your thoughts on teaching as well."

We continue to chat about teaching, mostly telling funny stories, for more than two hours as the sun sets on the horizon and the stars slowly replace the sunset. As the night grows darker, I notice Mark,

Olivia, and Jason are still talking at their table. I wish Carlos a good night and swing by my students' table to do the same.

"You OK, Morgan?" Mark asks, looking up at me.

"I'm OK," I say. "Sorry for not debriefing you all after that dive. I was just feeling pretty fatigued and hit my bunk. I also wanted to check in with Carlos this evening. I'm OK though…nothing a good night's sleep can't fix. We can catch up in the morning."

"You sure you're OK?" Olivia asks with a quizzical glance.

"Yeah…I'm fine," I say. "Oh, and congrats, by the way. You all completed the requirements to be advanced open water divers."

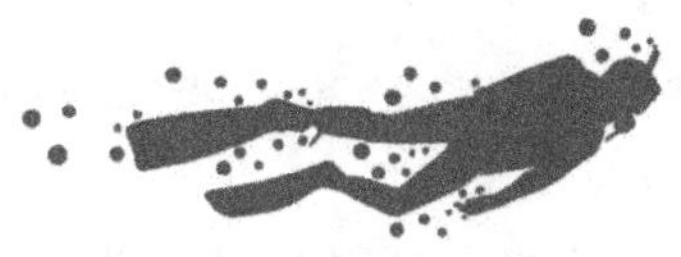

15

I awake on day eight, the last day of our trip aboard the *Hihi'o*. The sky is overcast as I make my way up toward the galley. Rain looks imminent, but it has not yet begun to fall. I get my morning cup of coffee and join Olivia and Jason at the regular table. Jason is reading what appears to be a book on philosophy. She has a Bible out. I notice it is open to the Gospel of Matthew.

"You've studied the Bible," Olivia says as I sit down. "Have you ever noticed the pattern to the way Jesus heals people?"

"Ok...let's just jump right into it with Morgan here," Jason says. He's been sitting with Olivia for what looks to be awhile, based on the bagel remains and cups collected on their table.

"Um...no," I answer. "I haven't noticed a pattern."

"Neither have I," Olivia says. "It was a trick question...there is no pattern to the way Jesus heals people."

Jason and I look at each other but say nothing. Mark approaches with a cup of coffee and sits with us. He also says nothing. His eyes are red and puffy. He rubs his head, further mussing up his short hair. He pulls the crumpled owner's manual for his dive computer out of his shorts pocket and begins to flip the tiny pages.

"Is there more to that?" I finally ask Olivia.

"Oh…sorry," she says. "I'm starting to sound like you…you know, a bunch of random thoughts that somehow turn into complete ideas at the end of the story."

"What the hell are you guys talking about now?" Mark grumbles. "More church stuff?"

"No," Olivia says, looking over at her dad. "Jesus stuff…not church stuff."

"What's the difference?" he asks, expecting no response.

"What's…the…difference," she repeats slowly. "There's a huge difference. For instance, church people have told me over the years that the Bible is the 'owner's manual' for our lives and that it gives us the 'blueprint' for living, like it somehow spells out every detail of how to live our lives…but Jesus never said that. In fact, many of his followers couldn't even read, much less have access to Old Testament scrolls. That's church stuff…something the church came up with that sort of sounds like Jesus, but not quite." She pauses again to collect her thoughts.

"And…" Jason says.

"Well, I mean, if that's true, then the Bible is the worst owner's manual I've ever read," she responds. The smile returns to her face as if she's thought of something funny. "Maybe the problem is the translation. You know how you get those owner's manuals for some electronic gadget that were translated into English from a foreign language...you know, the ones that don't make any sense? Maybe the Bible is one of those owner's manuals that lost something in the translation?"

As if on cue, Mark reads from his dive computer manual, "No-stop limits is to set plan mode on set computer. You mean like that?" He rolls his eyes, stands up, and walks over to collect his breakfast. Jason seems more curious, and I'm mostly just trying to wake up with some caffeine. Nothing is said as we all watch Mark return with his breakfast and sit down. He holds a fork in his right hand, computer manual in the other.

"The blueprint analogy of scripture just fails on so many levels," she continues. "I mean, good luck trying to build a life by exactly following every detail you find in the Bible. The greatest religious leaders of Jesus's day knew and practiced the written scriptures better than anyone, and Jesus said they completely missed the point of all of it. An architect friend of mine once told me the best blueprints are ones so well made that they require little or no dialogue between the architect and the builder. The best blueprint would answer every question the builder could possibly have about a construction project before he even asks it. The Bible, on the other hand, seems to be filled with all sorts of mystery, mixed messages, opinions that are not accurate, and outright contradiction. But what if God never designed the scriptures to answer every question we ever had about life? What if God never wanted us to use the Bible as the owner's manual to life? What if, instead, we're supposed to study it, then come directly to God with all our questions, concerns, burdens, that sort of thing? What if the Bible is God's word to us, but not in the way we think? What if it's more designed to get us to ask the right questions and seek out the *one* who inspired it versus trying to model our lives after the humans who physically wrote it down?"

Jason seems more engaged in this conversation than I would have guessed he would be. I'm still struggling to wake up and catch up to them. They've been awake longer than I have, and it appears they've been talking about this all morning. I'm walking in on their conclusions, but didn't hear all the conversation leading up to this.

"Interesting observation about the Bible, but what does that have to do with the pattern of Jesus's healing you asked about earlier?" I ask.

"I mean, sometimes he just tells people to go away and be healed, one time he packed mud on a guy's eyes, sometimes he says, 'your faith has made you well,' and sometimes people just touch him to be healed. I think the point to all of that is there is no pattern to healing. It can happen many different ways and we never know how, so we need to be open to whatever appears to be happening in the moment. Kinda like that bad owner's manual thing...there's no set formula. If there was, we could follow the formula and not Jesus. We could force others to act in a certain way to *fix* their problems, like you were talking about the other day, versus getting to know people and walking with them to a mutual conclusion."

Silence again in our small group. I'm not sure I completely understand what she's saying, but it sounds right. My mind drifts to diving. There are several principles that need to be followed in diving, but there are so many mitigating factors that each scenario has to be handled a bit differently. You should *learn the rules*, but diving is an odd brew of natural experience, technology, physiology, and pure science...something akin to the art of Michelangelo...the intersection of beauty, mystery, function, and knowledge.

"Enough of the Jesus stuff," Mark says. "Can we talk about our last day of diving?"

Olivia frowns as she looks at her dad. She told me she's convinced he has lost his faith and believes he will have joy again only when he finds it.

"Sure," she says. "Let's talk about diving."

"Are you diving with us today?" Mark asks me.

"I can if you want me to. Do you want to make your second deep dive today?" I ask, thinking about a grand finale to our trip.

"What else is there to learn?" Jason asks.

"A lot," I answer. "I'm still learning things about diving every time I go. But if you are asking about any sort of actual courses, one of the next logical steps would be the Deep Diver certification. Your Advanced Open Water Diver status means you're certified to dive to a hundred feet. The Deep Diver cert trains you to dive the entire recreational scuba diver range, which is up to one hundred and thirty feet. Beyond that, you are getting into the technical diver ranges that include more exotic breathing gases, planned decompression stops, and much more. You're a few hundred dives away from that type of diving."

"Can we do the Deep Diver certification?" Jason asks.

"We only have one day, but we can start it," I respond. "The deep dive from your Advanced Open Water course counts as one of the four deep dives you need to make for the Deep Diver certification. You need to make three more with an instructor for the actual certification. We have time for one more dive this morning before the boat returns to the dock, so you'd have to do two more with an instructor some other time."

"I'm game," Jason says.

"Let's do it," Olivia says. She and Jason both look at Mark, who says nothing.

"OK...we've moved further south down the Kona coast near Honaunau Bay," I say, "and we're anchored in about forty feet of water off the bow with the stern near a ledge that drops in a nearly vertical wall to two hundred-plus feet."

"I thought you said one hundred and thirty feet was the recreational diving limit," Mark says. I can hear the anxiety rising in his voice again.

"It is...in fact, we won't be going below one hundred and twenty feet, just as a precaution," I answer. "We will follow the anchor line to the bottom, then follow the slope of the seafloor down to the edge of a canyon at about seventy feet. We will then drop over the wall, down to one hundred and twenty feet. You'll have to pay close attention to the depth gauge on your computer because you'll be suspended next to the near-vertical wall with no bottom for a reference. So, as you know, the primary objective of every dive is for everyone to return safely. Then there are the secondary objectives ..."

I lay out the secondary objectives of their second deep dive by reading a few lines from the PADI instructor guide:

- *Execute a "free" descent using a reference line, wall, or sloping bottom as a visual guide only.*
- *Describe and record the changes that occur to three pressure-sensitive items while at depth.*
- *Perform a navigation swim with a compass away from, and back to, the anchor of the reference line....*
- *Perform an ascent using a reference line, wall, or sloping bottom as a visual guide only.*
- *Use depth gauge and timing device (or a dive computer with ascent-rate indicator) to measure an ascent rate not to exceed 18 meters/60 feet per minute.*
- *Perform a 3-minute safety stop at 5 meters/15 feet before surfacing without physically holding on to a reference line for positioning.*

"We'll gear up in thirty minutes and get ready for our last dive together," I conclude.

Olivia and Jason get up and walk off toward the bunk room to change into their swimsuits. I remain at the table with Mark.

"You got a second, Morgan?" he asks. He drops his computer manual on the table and sips on his fourth cup of coffee.

"Sure...what's up?" I say. I never quite know when or where he is going to want to talk, but this feels like one of those times.

"You just described my life when you talked about our next dive," Mark says.

"Not sure I follow," I reply.

"You know, my life...my life feels like I'm floating off an underwater wall, just trying to keep from sinking deeper...like if I sink any deeper, I'm not going to be able to come back."

I'm not sure how to respond, so I say nothing. He's processing something, and I don't want to interrupt his train of thought with a bunch of questions...but I definitely have a bunch of questions.

"Ever since Kate left me," he continues, "I feel like my life has been on pause...like I'm waiting to restart it someday. I know I need to process what happened, but I fear that if I let myself think about it too much, I'll just start spiraling into the deep."

"You really loved her, didn't you?" I ask.

"Yes...did and still do," he replies. "I always knew she was the one for me from the moment I met her. But then one day she wasn't."

He stops talking and stares through a starboard window of the salon. I look off in the same direction and see nothing out of the window but the same gray skies I saw earlier.

"I'm not the same person I was before my son died," I say, looking back across the table at Mark.

"You're what?" he asks, turning to look at me.

"I said I'm not the same person I was before my son died."

There's a look of confusion on his face as I'm connecting what he's saying to my own journey. He waits for me to say something more.

"I talk to a lot of men about their past marriages and failed relationships," I explain. "They often say that their ex had changed somehow and they didn't feel like they knew her anymore. Or that they had changed and could no longer relate to their significant other. I knew one couple where the wife had gotten sober and the husband had never seen her that way. In a weird, co-dependent sort of way he needed her to stay drunk because that's how he had learned to relate to her. Once she got her life together, it highlighted *his* shortcomings, which were part of the reason she drank so much. They wound up splitting up because he couldn't learn to relate to her in a new way…he couldn't change himself. After my son died, I told my wife Mary I actually could not remain the same person. I had friends who ultimately had to abandon me because they could no longer relate to this new person. I had to start over in many ways and construct a whole new person and life. The way my wife and I went about life, the way we thought about God, the way we related to other people was so different that I had to physically relocate to a completely different part of the country where almost no one knew me. I still haven't completely reconstructed my life, but at least my wife stuck it out with me. She changed a lot too. It was a transformational experience for both of us, and somehow we each found a way to relate to these new people we have become. I would say we're closer now in some ways, but neither of us would have made *that trade* knowingly."

"What trade?" Mark asks.

"The life of our son for a deeper relationship with each other and our other two kids."

We both sit staring off into space. The pain returns to both of us. The pain of loss, tinged with a new hope for a future. Tears come to Mark's eyes.

"That actually makes sense," he says.

"I'm glad it does to you," I respond. "I'm still not sure it makes sense to me. It's all so confusing."

"Can I sit with you two?" Olivia says, returning to the table.

Neither of us responds, so she sits down.

"Sorry, but I overheard what you said while I was standing over there talking to the chef," she says, looking at me. "You know…about what it means to become a new person. That actually does make a lot of sense."

Olivia shifts her gaze to Mark and continues. "I remember how different Jason was after he lost Matty. I remember watching you and mom struggle to relate to him or even know what to do. Watching Jason become a different person made you two different people. You always seemed a bit distant from each other to me, but now you were fighting. You never fought much before that...you just sort of lived separate lives in the same house. With Jason struggling, you were forced to deal with something together, and you didn't really know how."

She looks back at me. "The same thing happened when I came out...they didn't know what to do, so they fought, then ultimately stopped talking to each other. I think they both felt like they had made some big parenting mistake to make me the way that I am."

"That's pretty accurate," Mark says. "We were kinda roommates that lived pretty separate lives until there was something to argue about. We definitely didn't support Olivia's life choice. And when Matty died and Jason slipped into depression, we didn't know what to do. Olvia, you did more for him than either of us could do."

"*Could* do or *would* do?" Olivia asks as tears begin to form in her eyes. "I think there was a lot you *could* have done; you both just decided you *wouldn't* do anything...so you didn't. The same was true for my situation."

"You're right," Mark says. "I won't try to speak for your mom, but I was so wrapped up in my own shit, I didn't seem to know how to help anyone else."

"No one asked you to figure out how to help anyone else," she responds. "We just wanted you to be there for us any way you could. We weren't looking for guidance. We weren't looking for sage advice. Hell, we didn't really expect you to say anything. We just wanted you to stay...and you left." A tear runs down her cheek.

"I didn't really have a choice. She kicked me out," Mark says.

"Stop blaming her," Olivia says, raising her voice.

"Sorry. I'm not blaming her. Look, Olivia...I just...I'm not sure what to say."

"Don't say anything, goddammit...just put your arms around me and hold me like a father should. Just for once, shut your fucking mouth, stop trying to figure things out, and just *be* with me. I'm still hurting on so many levels from the way the community I grew up in treated me, and so is Jason. You'll probably never fully understand, and I'm not even asking you to understand. Just listen to me...really listen to me...and hold me.

Mark stands and takes Olivia's hand. He pulls her up from her chair and embraces her. She collapses into him like this is the hug she's waited for all her life...not an embrace of understanding, but an embrace of pure, unconditional love and acceptance. They stand that way for what seems like forever. I notice Jason on the other side of the galley, watching with a stoic expression, as if he's trying to decide if this love displayed by his father is real.

Olivia starts laughing and pushes her father away. "You're such a son of a bitch, but I can't help myself, I just need your love. It means so much to me."

"I'm sorry," Mark says.

"Sorry for what?" Olivia asks. They both collapse back into their chairs.

"For everything...but mostly for not being there for you."

"Now that the sob fest is over, can we go diving?" Jason asks as he approaches the table.

All three of them look at each other, then me. Again, I feel a bit self-conscious to be sitting in the middle of this family's reconstruction, but I dismiss the feeling, thinking instead about all that has transpired over the past several days. We didn't really know each other all that well before this cruise, but something has connected between us.

"Sure. Let's go diving," I say.

"That's your answer to everything," Olivia says. "Let's go diving."

"Yep," is all I reply. I stand up and walk to the aft deck to find my gear. I wipe my own tears with the back of my arm. The voice whispers, "Knowing is doing."

My three students follow me dutifully over the dive deck and begin prepping their gear for our dive. They are joking with each other as they prep. There is a connection between them that I had not noticed before this moment. The details of their lives had not really changed, but they were relating to each other in a different way.

As we continue to prepare, Jesus's words once again drift through my mind...

"Many will say to me on that day, Lord, did we not prophesy in your name and in your name drive out demons and perform many miracles? Then I will tell them plainly, I never knew you. Away from me, you evildoers!"

"I wonder if knowing people...I mean, really knowing people, including him, was what Jesus was talking about?" I ask the three of them. "Not so much trying to fix people's problems or what I think are their problems or getting people to follow a specific set of rules, but just unconditional love and sticking it out with people until an answer is found."

"More Jesus stuff?!" Mark says. "I thought we were going diving?"

"We are...but think about it. Was he teaching his followers to do as he did, but not to do so if it's for the wrong reasons...like if we do the right things, but for all the wrong reasons, we can end up causing more harm than good?"

"Behavior modification versus transformation," Oliva says.

"What versus transformation?" Jason asks.

"Behavior modification," Oliva repeats. "Trying to get people to do what I believe is right versus going on the journey of transformation with them...like Morgan here is always saying." She points her thumb at me. "You know how he's always saying that transformation is not about me trying to get you to change? It's about going on a journey together."

"Which is likely the biggest mistake many spiritual leaders make," I add, "thinking they have the right answers to everyone's problems instead of simply joining people on a journey of discovery. Jesus asked people to follow him, then they go on these journeys together and life just happens...teachable moments just happen."

"A beautiful dance, not an assembly line," Jason says. "So why don't people go on the journey together?"

"Because it's way harder to walk through life with people than it is to simply tell them what to do," I respond. "Jesus said 'Follow *me*,' not follow some sort of religion or set of rules. He also said his followers would 'know his voice.' There's a lot of mystery to all of it. What does it even mean to *follow* Jesus or *hear* his voice, especially now that he's not physically walking the earth? We can't figure it out, so we create religion...a set of rules to live by that we force other people to obey."

"People in my church say following Jesus means to repent of your sins and pray a specific prayer," Olivia says. "Oh, and then you have to make sure you don't do any of the *wrong* stuff. But Jesus never taught people to pray that prayer my church says you have to pray. There's also a lot of other things they say a follower of Jesus shouldn't do."

"Like marrying another woman?" I offer.

"Look, I know there's stuff in the Bible condemning homosexuality, mostly the Old Testament and the Apostle Paul, but it's funny that Jesus himself didn't seem to think it was important enough to even mention it. Or, if he did, his followers didn't think it was important enough to write it down."

"I always had a problem with that," Mark says. "It's why I eventually ended up outside the church. I never really bought the idea that some spiritual guru somehow knew what God wanted from me or was saying to me better than I did myself. I liked the relationships I had and the feeling they were just trying to prevent me from making mistakes, but it began to feel a lot more like they were trying to guilt and shame me into acting the way they wanted me to act. When I got divorced, there was no longer any place for me...nobody outright said that to me, but the message was clear. They were convinced I'd made mistakes, so I was out."

"I don't necessarily buy the idea that mistakes are bad," I say.

"That's not what I've been told," Jason replies. "How could mistakes be good?"

"Remember what I said the other day about comparing navigation to driving down the freeway?" I respond. "If you arrive safe and sound at your destination, after making a bunch of course corrections in your car, you wouldn't likely conclude that you're some sort of loser for having to make that many corrections. But, for some reason, it's easy to think of yourself as a loser if you have to make a bunch of course corrections in your life. What if that's what Jesus meant by 'follow me?' What if he meant just keep trying to figure out your life...don't just settle for where you are, continue to figure out where you're going no matter how old you are or how far you've come."

We all sit on the bench of the dive deck, strapped into our gear, sweating, and pondering what's just been said.

"So...let's go diving," I say.

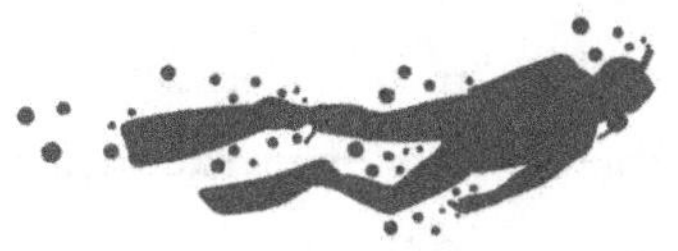

16

We stand on the dive deck, and I quickly reexplain the objectives of this dive. We do our predive safety checks and move toward the gate in the railing. The rain starts to fall as we plunge into the water. As we descend along the anchor line in the clear, blue water, I motion to our little group to look up. The rain dances on the surface of the water, sweeping by in sheets. We descend slowly along the anchor line. I encourage them to let go of the line and instead just use it as a visual reference. They all let go of the line and control their descent with their BCs, measured breathing, and fin kicking.

I stop short of touching the bottom and motion for them to follow me toward the edge of the drop-off. I then motion for them to set their compasses in the direction I am pointing. When everyone is set, we slowly make our way along the bottom until we reach about seventy feet deep. I can make out the edge of the drop-off where the water turns a much deeper blue. We continue kicking horizontally along the bottom until we all drop over the edge of the wall. We then turn upright in a vertical position and slowly allow ourselves to descend feet first. They all appear to have good control of their descent rate and stop descending at the predetermined one-hundred-and-twenty-foot mark.

I motion to each of them to ask if they are OK. They all give me the OK sign with their fingers. I pull out a small plastic tablet and prepare to have them one by one write their name in pencil underneath the spot where I had them write their names back on the boat. There will likely be a noticeable difference in their handwriting as they begin to experience the effects of gas narcosis. Narcosis, also known as "the rapture of the deep" and "the martini effect," typically starts affecting divers in noticeable ways at about a hundred feet. Like the effects of the consumption of alcohol (thus the martini effect), divers can begin to experience impaired judgment, impaired motor skills, giddiness, anxiety or a sense of euphoria, and overconfidence beyond a hundred feet. Beyond one hundred and thirty feet, the effects of narcosis can begin to get out of control, including confusion and hallucinations. At even more extreme depths, narcosis can lead to tunnel vision and blackouts. Narcosis within the recreational diving limit is usually manageable, so long as divers are aware they are being affected and continue to make rational decisions. To alleviate narcosis, divers can simply return to shallower depths, where the symptoms subside with no lasting effects.

As Jason begins to write his name, the effects of narcosis become clear. His handwriting is noticeably messier than it was at the surface. I also notice that as he focuses on his writing, he is losing control over his buoyancy and beginning to sink. Divers can often still focus on one task under the effects of narcosis but cannot tend to more than one task at a time, similar to being alcohol impaired. I gently pull Jason back up a few feet and take the slate out of his hands. I motion for him to maintain his depth, which he is able to do once I take back the slate. Olivia and Mark also have trouble controlling their depth while writing their names. I steady both of them as they write, and they take their buoyancy back under control as soon as I remove the slate from their hands.

Our time at depth expires quickly, and we slowly make our way back up the wall and onto the slope. As we are swimming back toward the boat, I notice a diver who is all alone. I look more closely and notice it is Andrea, one of the women who had prayed for me. She is on the boat with her husband Frank, whose name I'd made a point to learn last night. He is nowhere in sight.

As she searches frantically, I look toward the surface and see Frank hovering above her. He appears to be having trouble descending. I notice one of his weight pouches has fallen out of his BC and is lying on the seafloor. I pick it up and make my way toward her. Jason is ahead of me and trying to communicate to her. Just as I approach, Jason hands his alternate regulator to her and grabs onto her arm. She has run out of air while searching for her buddy, but Jason has plenty to spare. We abort our dive plans and make our way directly to the anchor line, where we begin our slow ascent. Jason has enough air to make a safety stop with Andrea breathing off his alternate air source, so we make the stop before continuing our ascent.

At the surface, Jason and I support Andrea as she orally inflates her BC by blowing into the mouthpiece. Frank is nowhere in sight, and I'm hoping he swam back to the boat. Back on the boat, Nate reassures me that Frank is back on board. I return the missing weight pouch to its owner and reunite the buddies, who are grateful to be together again.

Olivia is already wrapped in a towel as Mark, Jason, and I begin to peel out of our wetsuits.

"When you guys are done getting dressed, let's go in and have our final lunch together on the way back to the dock," I suggest.

With all of the divers back on board, the crew pulls the anchor, and our boat begins the twenty-mile trip back to the dock. We meet back inside and get in line for lunch, which appears to be a sandwich bar. Various types of bread, cheese, meats, and vegetables are strewn out on platters near a wide array of condiments and chips. We load up our plates and head back to the table.

"What happened on that dive?" Mark asks as we sit down.

"I noticed Andrea had lost her buddy Frank after one of his weight pouches fell out and he started floating toward the surface," I say. "I picked up the pouch and was heading toward Andrea to let her know what happened to her buddy. It appeared they were near the end of their dive, and during her search for Frank, she sucked all the air out of her tank. Jason noticed she was out of air and offered his alternate air source to her. Thankfully, she took it so we could all ascend safely together. His actions and calmness literally saved her life."

"You didn't even hesitate," Olivia says to Jason.

"I just saw she was in trouble and responded," he says. "It just felt like an instinct."

"Well, it was a good instinct," I respond. "I'm glad the training sunk in. You responded exactly as you should have. Most divers go a lifetime without encountering an actual emergency, so no one really knows exactly how they would react in that situation. But you reacted perfectly."

"I can't get over how smooth your response was out there," I say to Jason. "I've seen people who've been diving for years who probably wouldn't have responded that quickly. You have a natural ability for diving. You should think about going on and doing more. You'd be great with students."

"Thanks," he says. "But I'm not too sure I'd want to work like you do with people struggling to learn to dive. I'm more curious about going deeper. That one-hundred-twenty-foot dive got me curious about what's beyond there."

"There are lots of good instructors I know on the tech side of diving if you decide to go that route," I reply. "Just let me know."

"I, on the other hand, would be super curious to learn more about teaching," Olivia says. "It's so cool seeing that light turn on in other people's eyes when diving starts to click. I talked to Carlos's students for a long time to see how their class was progressing and could hear the enthusiasm in their voices. It really stuck with me."

"I can make that happen too," I say. "We should figure out a time to get together after this trip. I'm going to be back in California soon."

"What about dear old Dad?" Mark says with mock indignation. "Where do I fit in?"

"That's really up to you," I reply, "but I'd love to meet up for breakfast one of those days I'm in Orange County."

"I love the idea of growing more into this sport, even if my wife doesn't," Olivia says. "Just to see where it goes. Amy tends to just settle into the steady job and likes a quiet life."

"And you don't?" I ask.

"I'm not real interested in arriving...I prefer the trip. You know what I mean?"

"Not really," I say.

"Seems like people who believe they've somehow arrived just stop growing and really living," she explains. "I know my journey will require numerous corrections, like you said, so I just continue to respond to what I think is God's voice in my life and make those corrections until I reach my final destination someday when I'm dead."

"Nice try," Mark says, "but like I asked Morgan before, how do you know it's God's voice or just some random thought?"

"I've come to a place in my life where I'm convinced God is talking to me all of the time," I say. "Sorry...didn't mean to answer for you, Olivia."

"Go right ahead," she says, motioning with an open hand toward her father.

"I think he's talking to you too, Mark," I continue. "The real trick is actually listening and doing what you hear, then see how it works out. If you get it wrong, try again. It's easy to get caught up searching for answers in religion or other spiritual activities, but maybe God is simply telling you to just sit down in a quiet place and listen to his voice. I hear it all the time, but maybe for you it's more of a form of active meditation to block out all of the distractions."

"Knowing is doing," Olivia says.

I'm stopped cold. How did she know that? Did she hear the same voice I heard earlier today? I'm not sure what to say, but I'm freaking out a little bit.

"What do you mean?" I finally blurt out.

"Just seems like knowing and doing cannot be pulled apart," she explains. "They are two parts of the same thing. Knowing is doing and doing is knowing."

"That's the problem with the internet; too much knowing and very little doing," Jason says. "But how do I ever know for sure if something is from God or if it's something he wants me to do?"

"Take time to listen carefully, like Morgan said, however that works best for you," she answers. "Then do what you hear and closely observe what happens. If it seems like you heard it wrong, then listen some more, and try it again. You know, the little course corrections we talked about. For me, this journey of life is more about tuning into what's going on all around me and less about me trying to exert my will over life events or, even worse, people."

"You taught us a bunch of stuff, Morgan," Mark says, "whether you meant to or not."

"I did intend to teach you all the diving stuff," I reply. "But I'm also always fascinated how it gets translated to people's lives."

"So, do you have these kinds of talks with all of your students?" Jason asks.

"Oh, god no," I say. "This trip was pretty unusual. This stuff is always running through my head, but I don't come across a lot of students who want to dive into my thoughts as much as they do the ocean. You guys are definitely the exception."

"You just go as far as your students want to go," Olivia says. "That's my favorite quality about you…you're there to talk, but you're OK with people who don't want to talk."

The *Hihi'o* nears the dock, and the usual sadness mixed with longing drifts over me. Sad to see such a dynamic trip end but longing to get back to my family. The boat pulls into its slip, and the crew scurry off to tie up the lines. The captain comes over the loudspeaker to thank the divers for coming along and to remind them to tip the hard-working crew.

Andrea stops by our table carrying her gear and thanks Jason again for rescuing her. I look at him and wonder if he's thinking about his inability to save Matty. I know those two things don't somehow cosmically cancel each other out, but I do wonder how it affects his sense of self-worth.

We all stand and walk out onto the dive deck where all the divers are packing up the last pieces of their gear. We pack our gear in silence, standing side by side. Everyone I see has packed up and appears to be ready to rush back to their lives, except Jason, Olivia, and Mark, who don't appear to be in any hurry. We finally pack up and begin the long walk back to the parking lot.

"Let me throw my bags in my car, and I'll meet you back at yours to say goodbye," I say.

I stop at my car as I watch the three of them walk away. "There's more," the voice speaks to me. Some students become life-long friends; others return to their busy lives without much further contact. Some will never dive again. I'm hoping "there's more" means with these three.

I finish loading up and walk to their car. Olivia turns to me first.

"You're not done with me yet, Morgan," Olivia says, giving me a hug and kiss on the cheek. "You gave me your number...big mistake for you." She laughs and hops into the car.

"That was some trip," Jason says, reluctantly giving me a hug. "You taught me a lot. Now I gotta go sort through all of it. Thanks, John." Funny, he's the only one to use my first name. He climbs in behind the wheel.

"Couldna done it without you, Morgan," Mark says as he bear hugs me. "Thanks for your patience with this old dog."

"You know you're younger than me, right?" I ask.

"It's not the age, it's the mileage," he says, quoting the classic Indiana Jones line. "Anyway, I really appreciate all you did for me and my family. A lot of necessary stuff happened out there on the water...I think it was meant to be. So, thank you again."

"My pleasure," I say. "Truly I mean it...my pleasure. You guys taught me a lot too."

"Alright, enough of the sappy stuff," Jason says after rolling down the passenger window. "Let's roll."

Mark jumps into the passenger seat, and I watch them drive away.

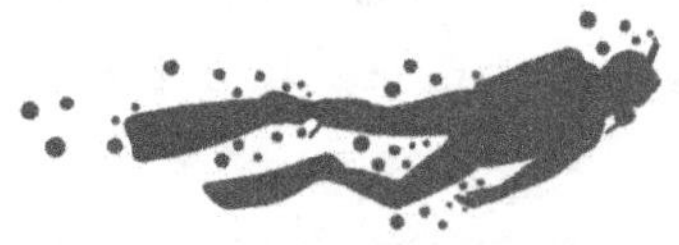

17

Months become a year before I finally make it back to Southern California from my home in Florida. We meet for breakfast at an old diner on a typically overcast June morning. By reputation, I expect the coffee to be marginal, the eggs bland, but the hashbrowns to be pretty good. There are not many of these places left in Orange County, and it takes me back to my childhood growing up amidst the never-ending orange tree groves from which the county once derived its name.

The groves have been replaced by planned communities, toll roads, freeway traffic, and Spanish tile roofs as far as the eye can see. As I'm seated, I think about how my birthplace has been transformed into something I no longer recognize...a bit like me.

Not all change is good, but change is inevitable, and to perpetually resist it doesn't seem like a life worth living. True transformation—becoming someone or something new—is a river with many bends through peaceful pastures, dangerous rapids, and over treacherous waterfalls. I had yet to decide whether I would continue to swim with the stream or resist the current and cling to the bank. The bounce in Mark's step and smile on his face as he walks through the door tells me he has decided to swim.

"Good morning," Mark says as he walks to my table.

"Good morning," I say, sliding out of the booth. "You're looking fit."

My compliment hangs in the air as an awkward moment passes between us. We are standing face-to-face after nearly a year apart. Mark has added a neatly-groomed, graying beard to his look and seems to have shed a few pounds. He extends his hand toward me. I begin to reach out to shake it. He changes his mind, slaps my hand away, and leans in for a hug. We embrace briefly, then take our seats across the table from each other.

"How have you been?" I ask.

"Not bad...not bad," he says as a server approaches.

We order coffees and scan the menu. Yesterday's breakfast clings to the edges of the sticky pages. He stares at me as if searching for something. I look down and read the breakfast specials, then glance up at the decor on the wall. There is a hodgepodge of spurs, cowboy hats, lariats, and other Western gear haphazardly screwed to the wall. There is vintage farming equipment—that may or may not be from the same era—hanging precariously on the other wall. All of it is coated in what appears to be years of dust. The decor makes as much sense as my relationship with Mark. We're very different people, and I'm still not convinced we would have been friends under different circumstances. Diving creates curious friendships. We've been bonded together through a common experience. He looks down at his tattered menu as I shift my gaze back to him.

"Thanks again for everything you did for us out in Hawaii," he finally says, looking up from his menu. "The instruction was great, and you were super patient with us...well...patient with me mostly."

"It was my pleasure," I reply. "I mean that literally...it was my pleasure. I love to watch students overcome their difficulties to become confident divers."

"I don't know if I'd describe myself as a *confident* diver, but I'm getting there. We've been doing a bit of shore diving around Laguna Beach and took a short trip back out to Hawaii to dive Molokini Crater off Maui."

"I love that spot," I say. "I haven't been there since my kids were little, but I remember enjoying all the life on that reef. My kids snorkeled around under the watch of the boat captain while Mary and I dove with the divemaster. We actually still know the divemaster all these years later. He now owns a dive shop on Bonaire in the Dutch Caribbean."

"Yeah, we had a great time there too," he says. "Although, Maui has changed a lot since I went there as a kid."

"Every place has changed a lot since we were kids," I reply. "But I've changed a lot too. I catch myself talking more and more about 'the good old days' as I get older. My kids tell me I talk a lot about how much better things used to be. I don't think I've ever convinced them though."

"Yeah, I do that too," he says. "But I'm trying not to."

He's left me an opening in the conversation to dive in a bit deeper. I start to say something, but I'm interrupted by the server returning with two cups and a pot of coffee. We watch as she pours us each a cup and walks back to set the pot down on the burner. We sit in silence as she returns to the table.

"Did you have time to decide what you want for breakfast?" she asks.

We both choose the "classic" breakfast of two eggs to order, bacon, hash browns, and toast.

"So, what's new?" I ask Mark.

"A lot is new," he says. "Got back into the gym, stopped drinking so much...watch what I eat ...I also actually reconciled a bit with Kate. She and Jack split a while back, and her new boyfriend was going through some stuff and got physically abusive with her, so she left him too. He tried to apologize, but she wasn't willing to risk being hit again. I wasn't the best husband, but I never got violent. I agreed with her that she deserved much better than abuse from her partner. I told her she should put him in jail, but she just wants to move on. Kate and I have gotten together a few times and had dinner once with Olivia and Jason. It was really nice for all of us to be together. Another time, when just Kate and I were together, we started talking about what happened to our marriage. We talked about how we had both changed so much since we were younger. I told her what you said about having a relationship that is flexible enough to handle change...how people change over the years or are even *transformed* by life into new people. It all seemed to make sense to her. She's not ready to go much further with me, but I'd get back together with her in a heartbeat. I never really fell out of love with her, I just forgot how to communicate it and never knew how to encourage her to grow. Like you said, I wanted the same *girl* I married and didn't know how to see her as a new person when life changed the both of us."

"Sounds promising," I say, sipping my lukewarm coffee. I make a mental note to never eat in this diner again. Mark is going at a pretty good clip, so I just listen.

"For some reason, learning how to dive with you changed the way I think about a lot of things. It somehow opened me up to the idea that an old dog could learn new tricks...that I can still grow as a person and even become something new. Kate commented that I seemed very different from when we were married. Olivia said it seemed like my confidence had returned, but not my ego. Seeing me embrace a more-humble approach to life and an eagerness to learn gave her new faith in me as her father."

"Wow. Sounds like a lot," I say. "I'm glad I got to play a tiny part in all of that."

"I don't know about tiny," Marks replies. "It may have been more than a tiny part."

The food arrives looking as bland as the previous diners' reviews had promised. We begin to eat. I look up at Mark, wondering at the depth of the changes in his life and what he said about an eagerness to learn. I've taught in many different disciplines over the years, and I teach scuba diving far differently from anything else, especially how I used to teach adult Sunday school. I had left the church, but I apparently never left Jesus's words behind. And a funny thing happened to me while teaching scuba...Jesus's words somehow came back through me, transforming my life and Mark's. His words once again peeled away layer after layer of the very structure of my life to get back to the core foundation on which it had been built. There are times in the past couple months that have been a pleasant walk in the park with God and times when life felt like surgery with no anesthesia. I notice Mark has paused to eat, so I jump in.

"These times of re-examination and learning are important for me," I say to Mark. "So that I can know my foundation is firmly planted on rock, not sand, before the next storm arrives."

"Yeah," Marks says, "You're sounding kinda churchy again. Kinda like that 'build your house upon the rock' thing Jesus said. Did you finally go back to church?"

I don't respond, adding some ketchup to my hash browns. I push the watery eggs to the edge of my plate. I'm not sure how to respond and, instead, wait for him to continue.

"I suppose the only way to really know where your foundation is built is to weather a storm or two," he says. "You know pretty quickly how real your faith is the moment the world and circumstances conspire to knock you down. I guess mine wasn't very strong because I abandoned all of it when my life went to hell. But I'm learning there is another way to know where my foundation lies before the storm arrives."

"Seems like the hardest part of building new things is letting go of the *good* things," I say.

"The *good* things?" he asks.

"I don't know...just that whole idea that I have to let go of *good* things for *great* things."

"Not sure I'm following," he says. "You're doing that thing you do...you know, where you start a conversation in the middle of a thought. Olivia and I joke about it. You have a point, but you seem to be the only one who knows what it is."

"Sorry. What I mean is most people understand giving up *bad* things in their lives for *good* things. But it's a lot harder to give up *good* things for *great* things. I heard someone say that good employees are the death of a creative business endeavor. If they're bad, you get rid of them, but if they're good, you keep them around, which leaves less room for *great* employees who really drive the business forward."

"Yes, but can't you push good employees to become great employees?" he asks.

"I suppose so, but it seems like you spend all of your time trying to motivate unmotivated people instead of searching for the best and inspiring them to do even greater things."

Mark thinks for a second about what I just said as he takes a bite of his toast. He doesn't appear to be buying what I'm selling.

"So, Kate invited me to go back to church with her," he says. "It's a different church than the one we went to together when we were married. She says they seem to be more *accepting* of people, and she really likes it, and I might like it too. I asked you before, but did you ever decide to go back to church?"

And there it is...the age-old question that Christians always ask... *where do you go to church*? The implication always seems to be that a true Christian always goes to church.

"No, I haven't," I say.

"Do you hate church?" he asks. "Did you have such a bad experience that you'll never go back? That's what Olivia told me."

"No, I don't hate church," I answer. "I just...I don't know how to explain it. I'm not sure how I fit into that paradigm anymore."

"Going back to church has helped me a lot lately," he says.

"I don't doubt it...but I also don't doubt that learning to scuba dive has been any less impactful on your life," I say, attempting to explain my earlier comment. "I don't believe that holiness or spirituality is restricted to church. I think it works for certain people in certain circumstances, especially young families, but I also believe holy moments occur everywhere in life and in ways that often don't look much like Sunday church. I just wonder sometimes if the model is broken."

"The model?" he asks.

"I worked in the newspaper business for a decade as a reporter, editor, et cetera, until eventually I was given the duty of moving the newspaper to the internet. The newspaper ethos up to that point was that *we* report the news and *you* read it. We will occasionally publish your letters reflecting your opinions, but the paper will primarily be *us* presenting news to *you*. I saw early on that if newspapers didn't embrace the idea that 'news' would be created by people outside of the official media to be responded to by other people outside of the media, then it would pretty quickly become irrelevant, and maybe even distrusted. Also, the financial model of printing words and advertising on actual paper could not keep up with a rapidly changing world of information. Newspapers are still around, but not many people under the age of fifty even look at them."

"So, you're saying churches will go the way of newspapers?"

"They already have," I say. "There are still some really big churches out there, but attendance has shrunk in proportion to the overall population. The way church happens mostly on a stage with a few key players while the congregation watches is an invention of humans trying to understand how to worship God. It worked for generations, especially when people couldn't read or understand the Bible for themselves, but I'm not sure the things that happen in churches on Sunday are as relevant to up-and-coming generations."

"Olivia is from one of those up-and-coming generations, and she still goes to church," Mark says. "They don't even approve of her lifestyle, and she still goes to church."

"You got me there," I say. "But Olivia seems to be the exception to many things."

"Now that you mention her, she asked if she could meet up with us...well, mostly you... after breakfast."

"She's here?" I ask, suddenly remembering my unfulfilled promise of planning to meet with her when I got to Southern California.

"Yeah, yeah," he says. "Well, not right here. She's down the street somewhere. She said she tried to text you but must have the wrong number."

I wonder to myself why she didn't get my number from Mark, but let it pass.

"She knew I was having breakfast with you this morning and asked if she could join us," Mark continues. "I told her no, but maybe she could meet up with us for coffee afterward. She said she just wanted to talk to you alone about something, so I told her to meet up with us after breakfast...she's waiting for me to text her."

"That's great to hear," I reply. "I'd love to see her too."

We continue eating breakfast, and the conversation turns back to the idea of *good* things versus *great* things.

"I've watched many people's lives kinda stop at good," I say. "Maybe they start with something bad and, over time, the bad thing is put away and a good thing comes out of it."

"You mean like breaking some bad habit...drugs...alcohol addiction... something like that?"

"Yes," I respond. "And other things too, like abusive relationships and unhealthy attachments. But far less often do I see people give up *good* things for *great* things."

"See, you lost me again," Mark says. He grimaces as he takes another sip of coffee. "This stuff is awful."

"I suppose I mean something deeper," I continue, sliding my cup out of the server's reach to avoid a refill. "Like some sort of passion that people have put off in their lives because what they already have is pretty good and they don't want to mess it up, like a stable family life, stable job, decent income."

"So, you're saying people should give up their family, job, and income for something else?

"Maybe...no...it's hard to explain. I think people know when there's some sort of greater calling in their lives. Something maybe they have put off for years or decades and maybe for good reasons. Maybe they had to follow a certain path to provide for their family, but now they are in a different place in their lives and some inner passion is still there. Maybe the whole idea of a mid-life crisis is there for a reason. I don't mean a young girlfriend or a flashy sports car... but maybe it happens to remind people they are more than just what they happened to have been doing the last several years."

"So, they should ditch their families and go chase some wild dream?"

"No, that's not what I'm saying exactly...but it might kinda look that way to an outsider," I answer. "What if you pursued that passion but *included* your family?"

"Not sure how that would work," Mark says. "Every time I tried pursuing my passion, I got further and further away from my family... just ask any of them. Speaking of family, look behind you."

I turn around and see Olivia walking in the door of the cramped diner. She obviously grew impatient waiting for a text from her father. She squints to adjust to the dark room and scans the tables. Her eyes land on me, and a broad smile crosses her face. "Transformation is a flood," the voice says.

"Damn…it's good to see you, Morgan," she says, approaching our table. She holds up her phone. "You gave me the wrong number."

I awkwardly slip out of our tiny booth and stand to greet her, still wondering why she didn't just get my number from her father. She gives me a bear hug, then pushes me away and gives me a once-over inspection.

"You're still pretty fit for your age," she says. "I think you could still pull it off."

"Um…thanks? Pull off what exactly?"

"I have this idea of something you should do, well, more like *we* should do."

"We, as in the three of us?"

"No, not him," she says, pointing at her dad. "We as in you, me, and my wife."

"Thanks!" Mark says sarcastically. "Always nice to be the *fourth* wheel."

"Oh, get over yourself," she says to him. He stands, and she gives him a kiss on the cheek. "Are you guys done with this breakfast thingy? I need to talk to Morgan here."

"Yeah, I suppose we are," Mark says. "You wanna go somewhere for another coffee?"

"Not with you," Olivia says. "I'll swing by the house later. I need to run something by John."

"So, you do know my first name," I say mockingly.

"Shut up, Morgan. I'm not done ditching my dad yet," she says with a devilish grin. As usual, she's running the conversation.

"Hey, well don't let me stand in the way," Mark says. "I'll pick up the tab here and the two of you can take a walk down the street."

He kisses Olivia on the cheek again and gives me a hug to say goodbye. Olivia and I start walking down the street. She puts her arm in my arm as we walk. Physical touch has never really been one of my so-called *love languages*—Mary's constant complaint—and public displays of affection are even more uncomfortable. I feel like strangers are staring at us, wondering why this older guy is arm in arm with this younger woman. I attempt to withdraw my arm, and Olivia squeezes tighter.

"You'll be fine, Morgan," she says. "Just go with it."

"Are we going someplace in particular?" I ask as we begin walking.

"Frankly, I don't give a shit where we go," she says. "I just need to ask you something."

"Again, with the salty language," I say in mock indignation.

"Oh, don't be an asshole," she responds. "We already had the bad language conversation. I am who I am."

"What do you want to ask me?" I'm beginning to get curious as to what's on her mind.

"Here," she says, motioning to a small coffee shop. "Let's go sit in here."

We go into the small coffee shop. It's a local spot, not part of a big chain. The staff is friendly, and it has a cozy atmosphere. I look around and wonder again why small business proprietors always seem to attach their odd collections to the walls. There is some sort of airplane theme going on. Olivia leads me to a table and goes to the counter to order a couple of coffees. I start to tell her what I want to drink.

"Oh, just shut up and go sit down," she says. "I'll order something you like...don't worry about it."

I'm slightly offended and pleased at the same time. Olivia is one of those people who has a way of bossing you around but making you feel happy about it at the same time. As I sit obediently by myself at the small table, I hear the voice beckoning me to let go of many *good* things so it can show me *great* things. I know what I hear, but I definitely don't see a path laid out for me.

"Uh oh," Olivia says, returning to the table with some sort of lattes. "You're thinking again. I can tell just by looking at you. What are you thinking about now?"

"I'm thinking about good versus great. I'm thinking about how I always have to give up the security of *good* things in order to go after *great* things."

"Perfect segue," Olivia says. "I need to ask you something...it's something you should do, and I want to help you...well, Amy and I want to help you."

"Who's Amy?" I ask.

"I never told you my wife's name?"

"No...at least I don't think so," I respond. "Well maybe...no... actually I think you did on the boat."

"Anyway," Oliva continues, "Amy and I have been talking about it and we think you should do some sort of a diving retreat. She's still too chickenshit to try diving, but she does marketing and has this whole idea about how it could work. She never gets excited about anything, so there must be something to it."

"To what?" I ask.

"A diving retreat," she repeats. "Have you ever thought about doing something like that? Kinda like our boat trip, but on purpose."

"But on purpose?" I repeat back to her while she takes a sip. I quickly recount how many great things have happened to me that didn't seem like they were on purpose...Mary, my family, business opportunities. On the other hand, becoming a scuba instructor was very on purpose.

"Yeah, a long time ago," I say, answering her earlier question. "I even had a name for it...*100 Feet Deep*."

"Ooh, I like it," she says. "Why haven't you done it?"

"Not sure," I say. "I could just never seem to pull the trigger... too much trouble finding a venue, working out the travel, cost, blah, blah, blah."

"So, you were going to take people to exotic locations and teach them to scuba dive?" she asks. "I wanna help get this going...so does Amy."

"Yeah, it sounds nice when you say it that way, but there are a lot of details that go into something like that. It's *actual* work and not much pay."

"C'mon, Morgan. You can do this, and we're gonna help. By the way, I'm going to become a divemaster. You're going to train me so I can help you teach. Let's go teach diving together during the day and transformation in the evenings."

I sit there staring into space. She's doing her mind-reading trick again. She's figured out my deepest desires—ones so deep I had forgotten them—and she's actually formulated a plan to carry them out. Did God somehow plant the same desire to see people grow in both of us? I had considered doing some sort of a dive retreat many, many years ago, but had mostly forgotten about it over time. I never could make it work out in my mind. Such a retreat would take up a lot of my time in planning and execution and take away from my day job.

After all, I still had my small companies to run, which performed business services for other small companies, such as videography, websites, accounting, payroll, human resources, etc. They were good businesses and provided for my family for many years. They put my children through college and always provided a steady source of income. To go off and do dive retreats was intriguing, but *way* too irresponsible. Were my businesses the *good* thing I needed to move past to get to the *great* thing... the thing that could change people's lives? Besides all of that, I was too old to start something new.

"He-e-e-ll–o-o-o," Olivia says. "You still here?"

"Oh...yeah...sorry," I respond. "I was just thinking..."

"Yes, I know," she says. "Time to stop thinking and start doing."

"But I don't have answers to people's problems," I say.

"We both know that, but like I told you on the boat, you're willing to take the journey with people. I'm not talking about a self-help seminar with you as the guru. All you gotta do is teach diving, and the rest just comes out if you make yourself available to people."

"You know what? You're right. It's time." Fear would no longer hold me back.

www.ingramcontent.com/pod-product-compliance
Lightning Source LLC
LaVergne TN
LVHW020713110826
845149LV00012B/2253